The
HIGH DEEDS
of Finn MacCool

Also available in

Red Fox Classics

Swallows and Amazons by Arthur Ransome

The Wolves of Willoughby Chase by Joan Aiken

Emil and the Detectives by Erich Kästner

Sword Song by Rosemary Sutcliff

Red Fox Classics

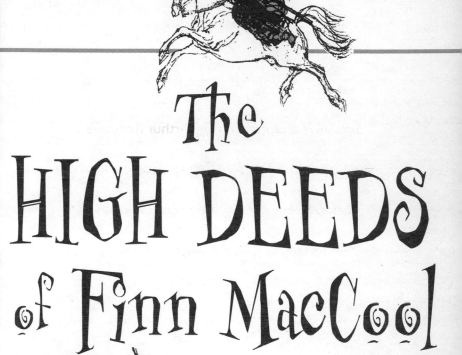

The HIGH DEEDS of Finn MacCool

Illustrated by Michael Charlton

ROSEMARY SUTCLIFF

RED FOX

A Red Fox Book

Published by Random House Children's Books
20 Vauxhall Bridge Road, London SW1V 2SA

A division of The Random House Group Ltd
London Melbourne Sydney Auckland
Johannesburg and agencies throughout the world

1 3 5 7 9 10 8 6 4 2

First published in Great Britain by
The Bodley Head 1967

This Red Fox edition 2001

Printed and bound in Great Britain by
Bookmarque Ltd, Croydon, Surrey

Papers used by The Random House Group Ltd are natural, recyclable products made from
wood grown in sustainable forests. The manufacturing processes conform to the environmental
regulations of the country of origin.

THE RANDOM HOUSE GROUP Limited Reg. No. 954009

ISBN 0 09 941422 8

www.randomhouse.co.uk

Contents

Author's Note

If you already know the stories of Cuchulain and the Red Branch Warriors, you will notice a very great difference between them and these stories of Finn Mac Cool. Both concern the adventures of Irish heroes, their loves and hates, their battles with strange and supernatural beings. Yet they belong to two quite different worlds.

It seems right and fitting that the Red Branch stories should be set in the wild harsh countryside of Northern Ireland. They are wild harsh tales. Their magic is darkly splendid, their people are very real, so that one loves and hates them and suffers and rejoices with them. They have the quality which we call Epic, which means that if we are deciding their right place on the bookshelves we should put them somewhere alongside Homer's *Iliad*, which is the greatest epic of all.

The stories of Finn Mac Cool belong to a later date, and are set in the South, many of them in the soft green Killarney countryside; and this again seems right and fitting. They belong, not to Epic, but to Folklore and Fairytale; and only here and there, as in the fighting for the river ford in *The Hostel of the Quicken Trees* something of the Hero Tale remains. The magic changes and shimmers and shifts on ahead of one, just a little out of reach, like the end of the rainbow. The Dananns, who in the Red Branch stories are still

recognizably gods or half-gods, have become the
Fairy Kind, with only a shred of their lost godhood
clinging to them here and there. Time means nothing
— Oisīn the son of Finn is a young warrior when *his*
son Osca is a young warrior. And in another way,
also, time means nothing. For the Lochlan Raiders,
whose battles with the Fianna come so often into the
stories, are the Vikings, the Norsemen; and the
Norsemen did not even begin to be sea raiders, let
alone reach the Irish coast, till long after Finn's day.
It is just that later story-tellers picked them out of their
own time and set them back five hundred years or so,
into Finn's, out of a feeling that the Sea Raiders were
the Enemy and therefore the right people for the
Fianna to fight.

The stories of the Fianna are full of loose ends and
contradictions, and unexplained wisps of strangeness
that seem to have drifted in for no especial reason
except that they are curious or beautiful and happened
to be floating by.

They are stories made simply for the delight of
story-making, and I have retold them in the same
spirit — even adding a flicker or a flourish of my own
from time to time — as everyone who has retold them
in the past thousand years or so has done before me.

ROSEMARY SUTCLIFF

1
The Birth and Boyhood
of Finn

In the proud and far back days, though not so far back
nor yet so proud as the days of the Red Branch Heroes,
there rose another mighty brotherhood in Erin, and
they were called the Fianna. They were a war-host
whose task was to hold the shores of Erin safe from
invaders, and they were a peace-host, for it was their
task also to keep down raids and harryings and blood
feuds between the five lesser kingdoms into which
Erin was divided. Ulster, Munster, Connacht,
Leinster and Mide had each their own companies of
the Fianna under their own Fian Chiefs; but one
Captain was over them all. And each and every man
must take his oath of loyalty, not to his own king, nor
to his own Fian Chief alone, but to the Captain and
to the High King of Erin himself, sitting in his high
hall at Tara with his right foot upon the Stone of
Destiny.

The Fianna came to their most full and valiant
flowering and to their greatest power in the time when
the hero Finn Mac Cool was their Captain, and
Cormac Mac Art, the grandson of Conn the Hundred-
Fighter, was High King of Erin.

But the story has its beginning back in the days of
Finn's father Cool Mac Trenmor, lord of the Clan
Bascna of Leinster, who was Captain before him, and

of Aed Mac Morna, Lord of the Clan Morna and Chief of the Connacht Fianna, who sought the Captaincy for himself.

At Cnucha, near where Dublin stands today, a great and bloody battle was fought between Clan Bascna and Clan Morna, as two bulls battle for the lordship of the herd. And one of Cool's household warriors wounded Aed in the eye, so sorely that he went by the name of Goll, which means one-eyed, ever after. But this Aed, who was now Goll Mac Morna, dealt Cool Mac Trenmor a still fiercer blow that cost him not the sight of an eye, but life itself, and he took from Cool's belt a certain bag of blue- and crimson-dyed crane-skin that was the Treasure Bag of the Fianna. And with the death of Cool and the loss of the Treasure Bag, the battle went against Clan Bascna, and there was a great slaughter, and those that were left of the Leinster Fianna, including Crimnal, the brother of Cool, as well as the Munster men who had stood with them, were driven into exile in the Connacht hills. And there was blood feud between Clan Bascna and Clan Morna from that day, which was to bring black sorrow upon Erin in the end.

News of the battle and of Cool's death was brought to his young wife, Murna of the White Neck, and she near her time to bear his child. And Murna, knowing that her lord's enemies would not allow any child of his to live after him if they could help it, fled, taking two of her most trusted women with her, into the wild fastnesses of Slieve Bloom. And there, like a hind lying up among the fern in the whitethorn month when the fawns are brought into the world, she bore a man-child, and not daring to keep him with her for fear of

the hunters on her trail, she called him Demna, and
gave him to the two women, bidding them bring him
up in the hidden glens of Slieve Bloom, until he was
of an age to fight for his rightful place as Cool's son.
Then, sadly, she went her way alone, and no more is
known of her save that at last, after many wanderings,
she found shelter with a chieftain of Kerry.

In the hidden glens of Slieve Bloom, Demna grew
from a babe into a child and from a child into a boy;
and the women trained him in all the ways of the wild,
so that by the time he was a youth, he was such a
hunter that he could bring a flying bird out of the sky
with one cast of a sling-stone, and run down the deer
on his naked feet without even a hound to help him;
and he knew the ways of wolf and otter, badger and
fox and falcon as a good hound-master knows the ways
of his own dogs. As he grew older he began to range
far and wide from the turf bothie that was all the home
he knew, and so one day he came to the hall of a great
chieftain, before which some boys of his own age were
playing hurley. The game looked to him good, and he
asked if he might join in; and they gave him a hurley
stick and told him the rules. And so soon as he got
into the way of it, he could play better than any of
them, even taking the ball from their best and swiftest
player.

The next day he played with them again, and though
they divided the teams so that a fourth of all their
number were set to play against him, he won the game.
The day after, it was half their number, and the day
after that, their whole number played against him, but
he won those games too. That evening in the hall, the
boys told the chieftain of the strange boy who had

joined them and beaten their whole double team at hurley.

'And what is he like, this boy,' asked the chieftain, 'and what is his name?'

'We do not know his name,' said the leader among the boys, 'but he is tall and strong, and the hair of him as bright as barley when it whitens in the sun at harvest time.'

'If he is as fair as that, then there's only one name for him,' said the chieftain, 'and that is Finn.'

And Finn, which means fair, he became, from that day forward.

The chieftain talked of the strange boy to a friend who passed that way on the hunting trail and lodged under the roof for the night, and the friend spoke of him to another, and so as time went by, rumours of his skill and daring spread like ripples on a pool when a stone is tossed into the water, until they came to the ears of Goll Mac Morna. And it seemed to Goll that if Cool had a son, he would be just such a one as this Finn . . . Murna of the White Neck had been heavy with child when she fled to the wilds; what if the child had been safely born and was a son? The boy would be fourteen by now, just coming to manhood. Goll Mac Morna smelled danger. He mustered the Connacht Fianna, and bade them hunt the boy down — they were great hunters as well as great warriors, the Fianna — and bring him back, living or dead.

But one of Finn's two foster-mothers was a Wise Woman, and she saw in a pool of black bog-water in the cupped palms of her hands how the Fianna of Connacht were hunting the hills for him. And she told the other woman, and together they spoke to Finn.

'The hunt is out for you, fosterling. Goll Mac Morna has heard more of you than is for your own good, and his men are questing through the woods to kill you, for you and not Goll are by rights the Captain of the Fianna of Erin. Therefore the time has come for you to leave the glen.'

Then Finn took the spear which they gave him, and his sling and his warmest cloak, and set out on his wanderings.

To and fro and up and down the length and breadth of Erin he wandered, taking service with now this king or chieftain and now that, and so getting his weapon-skill and his warrior training, against the day when he should stand out into the open and fight for his rightful place in the world. He began to gather to him a band of young men of much his own kind, fierce and gay and daring; and when he felt that the time was come, he led them into Connacht to seek out any of his father's old followers who might yet be living in the hills.

The day after they crossed the Connacht border, they came upon a woman bowed altogether with grief, and keening over the body of a young man outstretched on the stained and trampled grass.

Finn stopped when he saw her, and asked, 'What ill thing has happened here?'

She looked up at him, and her grief was so terrible that the tears falling from her eyes were great drops of blood. 'Here is my son Glonda, my only son, dead! Slain by Lia of Luachair and his followers. If you are a warrior as you seem, go now and avenge his death, since I have no other man to avenge it.'

So Finn went after this Lia of Luachair, and found him, and slew him in single combat, the followers of both standing by. And when Lia lay dead, Finn saw that a strange-seeming bag of crane-skin dyed blue and crimson was fastened to his belt. He knelt and untied the belt-thong, and opened the bag. Inside was a spearhead of fine dark blue iron, and a war-cap inlaid with silver, a shield with bronze studs around the rim, and a gold-clasped boar's-hide belt. Finn had no knowledge as to why the man should be carrying these things, but they looked worth keeping, so he put them back in the bag, and tied the thong to his own belt, and he and his companions went on their way.

Beyond the Shannon, in the shadowed depths of the

Connacht forests, he came upon a clearing in the woods, and in the clearing a cluster of branch-woven bothies; and as he looked, out from the low door-holes, one after another came old men, gaunt as wolves in a famine winter, bent and white-haired and half clad in animal skins and rags of old once-brilliant cloth. But each man carried in his hand an ancient sword or spear, for it seemed to them that the strange-comers could only be young warriors of the Clan Morna who had discovered their refuge at last; and they chose to meet their deaths fighting, rather than go down tamely without a blow. And something about their bearing and the way they handled their weapons even now, told Finn that they were the men he had come to seek, and he could have howled like a dead man's dog, thinking of the tall and splendid warriors that they had been on the morning that they stood out to fight at Cnucha.

Then he swallowed the grief in him and cried out to them with joy, 'You are the Clan Bascna! Which of you is Crimnal the brother of Cool?'

Then one of the old men stepped foward, sword in hand – and he not yet knowing whether or no he faced Clan Morna – and said fearlessly, 'I am Crimnal the brother of Cool.'

Finn looked in his old tired eyes, and said, 'I am Finn, the son of Cool.' And he knelt and laid the crane-skin bag at the old man's feet for a gift, since he had nothing else to give.

Crimnal looked at the bag, and cried out in a great voice to come from such a thin and bent old body, 'The Treasure Bag of the Fianna! Brothers, the time of our waiting is over!'

He opened the bag, and one by one drew out the things that it contained, the old men and the young men standing round to watch. And it seemed to Finn that the eyes of the old men grew brighter and their backs straighter and the grip of their weapon hands stronger with each object that appeared; the spearhead and the war-cap, the shield and the boar's-hide belt.

'Goll Mac Morna took this from your father's body after the slaying; and for eighteen years it has been lost to us. Now it returns again to Clan Bascná and with it will return also the lordship of the Fianna. Go you and take your father's place for it is yours, Finn Mac Cool.'

'Keep the Treasure Bag for me, then,' said Finn. 'My comrades I leave with you, to guard both it and you until I send you word to bring it out to me.'

And again he went his way, alone as at the first time.

But he knew that there was yet one more thing he had to learn before he was fitted to take his father's place; and he went to study poetry and the tales in which lay the ancient wisdom and history of his people with a certain Druid by the name of Finegas, who lived on the banks of the River Boyne.

Seven years Finegas had lived beside the Boyne, and all that while he had been striving by every means that he could think of to catch Fintan the Salmon of Knowledge, who lived in a dark pool of the river, where a great hazel tree bent its branches and dropped nuts of knowledge into the water. Fintan ate the nuts as they fell, and their power passed into him, and whoever ate of Fintan would possess the wisdom of all the ages. In seven years, a man — and he a Druid — may think of many ways to catch a salmon, but

Fintan the Salmon of Knowledge had escaped them all, until Finn came treading lightly through the woods to be the old man's pupil.

Soon after that, Finegas caught the Salmon quite easily, as though it had simply been waiting its own chosen time to be caught.

Finegas gave the Salmon to Finn to cook for him. 'And look that you eat nothing of the creature, not the smallest mouthful, yourself, but bring it to me as soon as it is ready, for it's wearying I've been for the taste of it, this seven long years past.'

Then he sat down in the doorway of his bothie, and waited. And a long wait it seemed to him. At last Finn brought the Salmon, steaming on a long dish of polished maple wood. But as he set it down, Finegas looked into his face, and saw there was a change in it, and that it was no longer the face of a boy. And he asked, 'Have you eaten any of the Salmon in spite of my words to you?'

And Finn shook his head. 'I have not. But when I turned it on the spit I scorched my thumb, and I sucked it to ease the smart. Was there any harm in that, my master?'

Finegas sighed a deep and heavy sigh, and pushed the dish away. 'Take the rest of the Salmon and eat it, for already in the hot juice on your thumb, you have had all the knowledge and power that was in it. And in you, and not in me as I had hoped, the prophecy is fulfilled. And when you have eaten, go from here, for there is nothing more that I can teach you.'

From that day forward, whenever Finn wished to know how some future thing would turn out, or the meaning of some mystery, or to gain tidings of events happening at a distance, he had only to put his scorched thumb between his teeth and the knowledge would come to him as though it were the Second Sight.

And another power came to him also at that time, so that he could save the life of any sick or wounded man, no matter how near to death, by giving him a drink of water from his cupped hands.

2
How Finn won his Father's Place

Now, when he left his Druid master beside the Boyne, Finn knew that the time was fully come for him to be claiming his father's place, and he set out for Tara of the High Kings.

It was Samhein, the time of the great autumn feast, and as he drew nearer, his road, and the four other roads that met at Tara, became more and more densely thronged with chiefs and warriors, on horseback or in chariots decorated with bronze and walrus ivory, with their women in gowns of green and saffron and crimson and heather-dark plaid and the golden apples swinging from the ends of their braided hair, and their tall feather-heeled hounds running alongside. For at Samhein all the kings and chiefs of Erin came together, and all men were free to sit at table in the High King's hall if they could find room — and so long as they left their weapons outside.

So up the Royal Hill and in through the gate, and across the broad forecourt went Finn, amid the incoming throng, and sat himself down with the King's household warriors, ate badger's meat baked with salt and honey, and drank the yellow mead from a silver-bound oxhorn, and watched the High King and the tall scarred man close beside him, who he knew from his lack of an eye must be Goll Mac Morna, and waited for the King to notice that there was a stranger among his warriors.

And presently the High King did notice him, and sent one of his court officials to bid him come and stand before the High Table.

'What is your name? And why do you come and seat yourself unannounced among my household warriors?' demanded the King.

And Finn flung up his pale bright head and gave him back stare for stare. 'I am Finn the son of Cool who was once Captain of all the Fianna of Erin, Cormac High King, and I am come to carry my spear in your service as he did; but for me, I will carry it in the ranks of your household warriors, and not with the Fianna.' This he said because he knew that to join the Fianna he would have to swear faith to Goll Mac Morna, and he was no light faithbreaker.

'If you are the son of Cool, then you may be proud of your birth,' said the King. 'Your father was a mighty hero, and his spear I trusted as I would trust my own — and as I will trust yours.'

Then Finn swore faith to Cormac the High King; and Cormac gave him a place among his household warriors, and the feasting went on as it had done before, and the King's harper beat upon his curved harp while the mead horns passed from hand to hand, and the great hounds fought over the bones among the rushes on the floor.

But little by little the drink began to pass more slowly, the laughter grew fitful and the harp-song fell away, and men began to half glance into each other's eyes and break off the glance quickly, as though afraid of what they might see.

And indeed they had good reason.

Every Samhein for the past twenty years, Tara had been weirdly and terribly visited. Fiend or Fairy no one knew what the strange-comer was, only that his name was Aillen of the Flaming Breath, and every Samhein at midnight he came upon them from the Fairy hill close by, and burned the royal dun over their heads. No use for any warrior, however valiant, to try to withstand him, for he carried a silver harp, and as he came he drew from its strings the sweetest and most drowsy music that ever breathed upon the ears of men, and all who heard it drifted into a deep enchanted sleep. So each Samhein it was the same; he came upon Tara with no one left awake to withstand him, and he breathed where he would with a licking breath of fire until thatch and timber blackened and scorched and twisted, and kindled into leaping flame. So every year Tara must be rebuilt, and every year again — and yet again.

When the sounds of feasting had died quite away, and an uneasy hush with little stirrings and little eddies in it held the King's hall, Cormac rose in his High Place, and offered a mighty reward in gold and horses and women slaves to any warrior who could prevail against Aillen of the Flaming Breath, and keep the thatch on Tara till the next day's dawn. He had made the same offer, and his father before him, twenty Samhein nights, and after the first few times, no man, not the boldest of his warriors, had come forward to answer, for they knew that neither courage nor skill nor strength would avail them against the wicked silvery music. So Cormac made the offer, and waited, without hope.

And then Finn rose in his place, and stood to face the troubled King. 'Cormac Mac Art, High King of Erin, I will forgo the gold and the horses and the women slaves, but if I prevail against this horror of the night, and keep the thatch on Tara till tomorrow's dawn, will you swear before all these in your hall to give me my rightful heritage?'

'It is a bold man, I'm thinking, who seeks to bargain with the High King,' said Cormac. 'What heritage is that?'

'The Captaincy of the Fianna of Erin.'

'I have given you the place that you asked for among my own warriors,' said Cormac, 'and is that not good enough for you?'

'Not if I keep that thatch on Tara,' said Finn.

Then a murmur ran round the hall, and men looked at each other and at Goll Mac Morna, who sat looking straight before him with his one bright falcon's eye.

'I swear,' said the King, 'and let all those gathered here, the kings and chiefs of Erin, warriors of my household and of all the Fianna, witness to my swearing. If you overcome Aillen of the Flaming Breath, you will have earned the Captaincy in your own right, and in your own right, as well as by heritage, you shall hold it.'

So Finn left the King's hall, and took up his spear that he had laid by when he entered, and went up to the rampart walk that crested the encircling turf wall. He did not know at all how he should succeed when so many had failed before him, but his faith was in his destiny, and he did not doubt that he would prevail. And while he paced to and fro, waiting and watching, and listening more than all, one of the older warriors came after him, carrying a spear with its head laced into a leather sheath.

'Long ago your father saved my life,' said the man 'and now is the time to be repaying my debt. Take the spear, to aid you in your fight.'

'I have a good spear of my own,' Finn said.

But the other shook his head. 'Not such a spear as this, that must be kept hooded like a hawk lest it run wild and drink blood of its own accord. It was forged by Lein, the Smith of the Gods, and he beat into it the fire of the sun and the potency of the moon. When you hear the first breath of the fairy music, lay the blade to your forehead, and the fierceness and the bloodlust in it will drive away all sleep from you. Take it.'

Finn took the spear and loosed the thongs and slipped off the cover. He saw a spearhead of iron as sheeny-blue as the moonlight, and studded with thirty rivets of bright Arabian gold.

'Take it,' said the man once more.

And Finn hooded the spear again, but left the thongs loose. And carrying it, he returned to his pacing up and down, looking always out over the plains of Mide, white under the moon, and listening, listening until the silence in his own ears sounded loud as the hushing of the sea in a shell.

And then it came, the faintest gossamer shimmer of distant harp-music. Nearer and clearer, even as he checked to listen, clearer and nearer; the fairy music lapped like the first gentle wavelets of sleep about him. It was the light summer wind through the moorland grasses of Slieve Bloom, it was the murmur of bees among the sun-warmed bell heather; it was all the

lullabies that ever his foster mothers had sung to him
when he was too young to remember . . .

Finn tore himself free of the enchantment that was
weaving itself around him, and with fingers that
seemed weak and numb, dragged the leather hood
from the spear and pressed the blade to his forehead.
Instantly he heard the voice of the spear more clearly
than the voice of Aillen's harp; an angry hornet note
that drove all sleep away from him. His head cleared,
and looking out once more towards the Fairy hill, he
saw a thing like a mist-wraith floating towards him
along the ground. Nearer and nearer, taking shape and
substance as it came, until Finn was looking at the pale
airy shape of Aillen of the Flaming Breath, so near and
clear now that he could even catch the silver ripple of
the harpstrings on which the thing played with long
white fingers as he came. Now Aillen had reached the
stockade which crowned the turf walls, and a long
tongue of greenish flame shot from his mouth and
lapped at the timbers.

Finn tore off his mantle of saffron-dyed ram skins,
and with one sweep of it, beat the flame into the
ground.

With his flame beaten out, Aillen gave a terrible
wailing cry, and turned over and back, streaming
through himself like a wave flung back by a rocky
shore, and fled away towards the Fairy hill. But Finn,
with the hornet-shouting of the spear loud and urgent
in his ears, leapt the stockade and was after him, as
swift as he.

The doorway of the Fairy hill stood open, letting out
a green twilight, and as Aillen fled wailing towards it,
Finn made one mighty cast with the spear, and the

spear flew on its way rejoicing, and passed through the creature's body and out at the other side. And there

on the threshold of the Fairy hill — or where the threshold had been, for now the door was gone, and only the frost-crisped grass and brambles gleamed faintly under the moon — Aillen of the Flaming Breath lay dead, like a heap of thistledown and touchwood and the fungus that grows on the north side of trees, tangled together into somewhat the shape of a man.

Then Finn cut off the head and set it on the point of his spear and carried it back to Tara and set it up on the walls for all to see.

When morning came, and Tara still stood as it had stood last night, all men knew that Finn must have prevailed against Aillen of the Flaming Breath, and led by the High King they went out to the ramparts; and there they found Finn leaning wearily on the stockade and waiting for their coming, and nothing to show for the happenings of the night but the scorch marks on his saffron cloak which he had wrapped close about himself against the dawn chill, and the strange and ghastly head upreared on his spear point against the morning sky.

'I have kept the thatch on Tara,' Finn said.

Then Cormac Mac Art set his arm across the young man's shoulders, and turned with him to face the mighty gathering in the forecourt below. 'Chiefs and kings and warriors, last night ye bore witness when I swore in the mead hall that if this Finn son of Cool should prevail against Aillen of the Flaming Breath, I would set him in his father's place as Captain of the Fianna of Erin. Last night it was in my mind that it was small chance he had, where so many had failed before. But he has prevailed; he has slain the fire fiend and saved Tara, and therefore I give him to you of the Fianna for your Captain, according to my word and yours. Any of you that will not serve under him, let you leave Erin, freely and without disgrace; there are other war bands and kings' bodyguards overseas in other lands.' He turned to the tall one-eyed man who stood out before the rest. 'That is for you also, Goll Mac Morna, for you who have been the Fian Captain these eighteen years past. Will you strike hands with Finn Mac Cool, and lead the Connacht Fianna under him? Or will you cross the sea and carry your sword into the service of another king?'

'I will strike hands with Finn the son of Cool my old enemy,' said Goll Mac Morna, though the words stuck a little in his throat, and he and Finn spat in their palms and struck hands like two men sealing a bargain.

No man went out from the High King's forecourt to carry his sword overseas, and the feud between Clan Morna and Clan Bascna, though it was not healed, was skinned over and remained so for many years to come.

So Finn Mac Cool became Captain of the Fianna of Erin, as his father had been before him.

3
Finn and the Fianna

It is time to tell something of the Fianna and the life
they lived. In peace time it was like this: in winter they
went to their own homes, or assembled in the halls of
some greater chieftain, and in the summer they
gathered for training, whole battalions of them living
together in the open, sleeping in branch-woven cabins
if they slept under cover at all, or out on the bare
mountain-sides with no cover but their cloaks between
themselves and the grey dew, and living off the land
wherever they might be. The hunting was rich, for in

those days much of Erin was fleeced with forest, and
in the forests ran boar and wolf and red deer. The
Fianna were famous as hunters as well as warriors;
sometimes on horseback, sometimes on foot, they
hunted with their great wolfhounds who stood as tall
at the shoulder as a yearling colt, and the hounds were
not more fleet-footed than their masters. It was said
that in a single day's chase, they could hunt from

Killarney in Kerry to Ben Eader near the East coast, climbing the mountains and cutting across the trackless bogs with no more thought of a check or a way round, than if they had been the Wild Hunt itself.

Finn's boyhood among the wild glens of Slieve Bloom had fitted him for this life as no other kind of boyhood could have done. He knew the ways of all furred and feathered things. He could make the cry of a dog-fox so truly that a vixen would answer him; he could move through the forest with no more sound than a shadow makes in moving.

Many — very many — years after his death, his son Oisín, who was a poet and a harper as well as one of the greatest of his warriors, told of him in a song, that Finn's favourite music was,

'The babble of wild duck on the lake of the three
    narrows,
 The scolding talk of the blackbird of Derry cairn.
 The cattle lowing in the Glen of the Thrushes.'

And again, in another song:

'These are the sounds that were dear to Finn —
    The din of battle, the banquet's glee,
 The bay of his hounds through the rough glens ringing
    And the blackbird singing in Letter Lee.

'The shingle grinding along the shore
    When they dragged his war-boats down to the sea;
 The dawn wind whistling his spears among
    And the magic song of his minstrels three.'

Many things were told of Finn by the warriors who served under him, for he was such a Captain as men will tell of to their grandsons, and their grandsons' grandsons pass on the tale. It was told of him that his sense of justice was so sure and so unbreakable that if he had to give judgement in a quarrel between a stranger and his own son, he would be as fair to the stranger as to his son — and as fair to his son as to the stranger. It was told of him that he was so generous that if the leaves falling from the trees in autumn were gold and the foam on the salt sea waves was silver, Finn would give it all away to any who asked him. It was told of him also that he had another side, a dark-of-the-moon side, and could forgive an injury, laughing, but knew also how to nurse an old hate through the years, to the death of the man he hated.

This was the new Captain of the Fianna of Erin, with nothing yet told of him at all save his wild boyhood deeds, and that he had overcome Aillen of the Flaming Breath and that he was the son of Cool Mac Trenmor.

And now, Finn Mac Cool must have a living place, a great hall and strong point where he could gather his chief warriors about him. So Cormac the High King gave him the strong Dun of Almu, in Kildare. Today the place is called the Hill of Allen, and there is nothing to be seen there but the wave-lift traces of encircling turf banks under the heather and bramble-domes, no sound but the wind blowing over and the green plover crying; but when Finn was its lord, the hill was circled by massive walls of turf and timber, gleaming white with lime-wash the hall standing high and mighty above the byres and barns and chariot sheds and the sleeping-places of warriors; and the weapon stone stood tall in the forecourt and many proud chiefs and champions sharpened their weapons on it in time of war.

Of these champions, the kin and the hearth-companions of Finn Mac Cool, the foremost and hardest fighter despite his one eye, was his old enemy Goll Mac Morna, a hero savage as a wild boar to his foes, staunch and faithful to his friends.

Then also, there was Conan, son of that lord of Luachair whom Finn had slain with the Treasure Bag of the Fianna upon him, and who, for seven years after his father's death, was an outlaw, raiding against the Fianna, slaying here a man and there a war dog, firing the thatch of a chieftain's hall. Conan Mac Lia stole at last upon Finn himself when he chanced to be alone after a day's hunting, and flung his arms round him from behind in a grip so strong that it could hold even the Fian Captain fast and motionless. Finn knew that there was only one man in Erin strong enough to do that, and he said, 'What do you want of me, Conan Mac Lia?'

'To swear fealty to you, and carry my spear among the Fianna, for I am weary of playing wolf on your flanks.'

So Finn laughed and said, 'As you will, Conan Mac Lia. Let you keep your faith with me and I will keep mine with you.' So Conan swore fealty and served loyally with the Fianna for thirty years.

Then there was another, Conan of the Clan Morna, a fat man growing bald, no great fighter but great at belittling other men's deeds. No man had much liking for Conan Maol, but Finn kept him with him because he had a hard core of common sense and his advice was often worth listening to. It was told that when he was stripped he showed a black ram's fleece down his back instead of human skin, and this is the way he came by it. One day when Conan and some others of the Fianna were out hunting they came upon a stately dun, with walls lime-washed as white as a war shield, and roofs of many-coloured thatch, and being hungry and weary they entered in search of hospitality. They found themselves in a chieftain's hall with silken hangings and pillars of cedar wood upholding the roof. There was no sign of any living creature, man, woman, child or hound, but in the midst of the hall a table was set for a feast, with boar's flesh and venison, yew-wood vats of crimson foreign wine and drinking cups of gold and silver. They set themselves down to eat and drink, stretching weary legs beneath the table, and cheerful as groomsmen at a wedding feast. But midway through the meal, one of them sprang to his feet with a startled cry of warning, and as the rest looked up, they saw the place changing around them, the walls to rough wattle, the fine thatched roof with its painted rafters to smoke-blackened turf such as might cover a herdsman's bothie!

'Enchantment!' someone cried out, and they all sprang to their feet, making for the doorway which was shrinking to be no bigger than the mouth of a fox's earth. But Conan was still so busy with the food and drink that he noticed nothing of this until they shouted to him; and then, when he woke at last to his danger, and tried to rise and follow, he found himself stuck to his chair like a bird caught in lime. Terrified now, he howled to them for help, and two of them rushed back and seized him by an arm each, and pulled with all their might. They tore him free, but in parting from his chair, he left behind the better part of his tunic and breeks and all the skin of his back and hams. They hauled him through the narrowing doorway and laid him face down outside, wailing like a banshee with the pain of his hurts.

Then, for they could think of nothing else to do for him, they brought a black ram from a man herding his flock on the next hill, killed and flayed it, and clapped the skin upon Conan's raw back. And there it took root and grew, and was with him to the day of his death.

Another of the Fianna was Keelta Mac Ronan, famous for his fleetness of foot. It was himself that ran down and slew a wild boar which the Fianna had hunted for years without being able to touch so much as a bristle of its ugly hide. He had the gift of minstrelsy, and there were few who the Fianna liked better to listen to after supper when the mead jars went round and it was time to wake the music of the harp. Unless of course it was Oisín, in later years, for there was never a harper to touch Oisín, who could play and sing the very larks out of the blue sky.

There was Ligan Lumina, Ligan the Leaper, who could overtake the west wind, and leap across Tara from side to side when the lightness of heart was on him; and Fergus Finvel, who was among the wisest of Finn's councillors; and there was Dering, son of Dobar O'Bascna, who could tell by shutting his eyes and looking into the darkness at the back of his head what things were happening at a distance or would happen at a future time.

There was Dearmid O'Dyna, who was brave and

gentle and so fair to look upon that few women could look and not fall in love with him.

And there were the few old warriors from the Connacht woods and their young bodyguard, who came with the Treasure Bag of the Fianna. The old warriors were past their fighting days, but they sat beside the fire at Almu in winter and in the sun before the hall door in summer and plagued the young ones with their counsel.

And in the later days, when Finn himself was growing old, there was Osca, Oisīn's son, the bravest of the brave, who seemed born and bred for fighting and for nothing else, but a loyal and loving friend to one man, and that man Dearmid O'Dyna. For Dearmid's sake, there came bad blood between himself and Finn in the last years of all; yet another of the things told of Finn was that he wept only twice in all his life, and once was for the death of Bran, his favourite hound, and once was for the death of Osca.

These then, were the greatest and most famous of the champions who followed Finn Mac Cool, but there were many and many more, whose names have been forgotten, for indeed the Fianna of Erin was more than three thousand strong. And scarce a day went by that a man did not come seeking to join it.

Strange men, some of them, with strange stories at their backs, such as the three young warriors with the great hound. The hound had this power, that by breathing on water he could change it into wine or mead, whichever was demanded, and his three masters made the condition, on joining the Fianna, that they should always sleep apart from the rest of the camp, and when Finn enquired why this might be, the leader among them explained, 'Every night, one of us three must die, and the other two must watch beside him till he returns to life at sunrise. Therefore we would be undisturbed in our watching.'

It was not easy to join the Fianna, and many tried and failed, for Finn ruled that no man should become one of the proud brotherhood without passing many tests. A warrior must be skilful as well as brave, and to prove his skill, the young man who wished to join their number must first, with only a shield and a hazel rod, defend himself against nine men posted all around him while standing in a hole in the ground, so that he could not move from the hips down. If one of the spears they cast at him so much as grazed his skin or drew one drop of blood, he was not taken. Then his hair was plaited into a score of braids, and he was hunted through the woods by others of the Fianna; and if he was wounded or run down, if his spear trembled in his hand, or a single strand of hair broke loose from its braiding, or if a dry twig cracked under his running foot, he was not taken. Then he must leap over a branch set at his own height above the ground, and run under another set level with his knee, and still running he must pull a thorn out of his foot without slackening speed. If he passed all these tests, he must still know the Twelve Books of Poetry, and be able to recite long passages from them; and he must have by heart a score or more of the ancient tales in which was hidden the secret lore and history of Erin. And if he could do all these things, he was taken.

Then Finn would bind him by oath never to take a dowry with a wife, never to take another man's cattle by raiders' right, unless in vengeance for a wrong, never to refuse help to any man, and never, however hard pressed, to fall back in combat before less than nine warriors.

And then at last the newcomer would swear fealty to the High King of Erin, and to Finn Mac Cool his Captain. And after that he took his place among the Fianna.

And so it was that in the time of Finn, the Fianna came to its full greatness such as it had never had before. And with the death of Finn its greatness passed away.

4
Finn and the Young Hero's Children

This story and the one that follows it tell how Finn
Mac Cool came by the two hounds that were his
favourites among all his hunting dogs, and it starts in
this way.

Finn and some of his companions were out hunting
among the seaward hills of Argyll. In those days
Argyll was close kin to Erin and many of the great
chiefs hunted on both sides of the water. They had
killed, and were resting in the warm honey-smelling
heather that crept right down to the rocky shore where
the little waves of fine weather came in from the West,
to cream upon the gull-grey shingle. And as they
sprawled at their ease, Goll Mac Morna, whose one
eye was better than most men's two, said to them
suddenly, 'Look there!' And when they looked where
his finger pointed out to sea, they saw a dark fleck on
the distant brightness of the water, that became a nut-
shell boat, that became at last a fine war-galley pulling
in to shore.

The men with Finn caught up their hunting spears
at the sight. But Finn said, 'Ach now, let you wait!
Every stranger is not an enemy, and there are no war
shields hung along the side of the galley.'

The boat grounded on the shingle, and the tall man
at the steering oar sprang overboard, and leaving the
rowers to run her further up the beach, he turned his

face to the land, and came striding up through the salt-burned heather to where Finn and his companions stood waiting for his coming.

He was tall and finely dressed, with strings of coral and twisted silver about his neck, but his eyes under his golden brows were dark with trouble as they moved from one to another of the Fian hunters until they found and rested upon Finn.

'You are Finn Mac Cool, the Lord of the Fianna?' he said.

'I am so,' said Finn. 'What is it that brings you seeking me?'

'I come asking for your help to save my child, for without it, I shall lose this small one as I have lost two sons before.'

'And how did this grief come upon you? And what thing can I be doing about it?'

'As to both these questions, they can wait. Believe only — for it is true — that you and only you can save this third child for me and my wife.'

'And how if I refuse to go on a blind errand?' Finn said.

'Then I lay this geise upon you, that before you eat or drink or sleep, you follow me,' said the stranger. And turning, he strode away down to the shore.

His crew saw him coming, and before he reached it they had run the war-boat down into the shallows once more. He sprang in, the rowers after him; they bent to their oars and the galley drew away from the shore, becoming first a nut-shell boat, then a splinter of darkness far out on the bright water, then gone as though it had never been.

And Finn turned from looking after it and said,

'Since I may neither eat nor drink nor sleep until I follow, it is in my mind that now I had best be following.'

'We will come with you,' said his companions, but Finn refused and bade them carry the kill back to the hunting camp, and he went down to the shore alone.

Among the rocks and the spray-wet shingle he met seven men, who might almost have been waiting for him. 'Greetings to you, Finn Mac Cool,' said the first. 'The sun and the moon on your path. Is there a service that we can be doing you?'

'Greetings to you,' said Finn Mac Cool. 'What thing can you do best in all the world?'

'I am a shipwright,' said the man.

'How good a shipwright are you?'

'With three strokes of my axe I can fell the alder tree that grows yonder where the stream comes down, and cut it into planks and build a ship of them.'

'That is a good skill,' said Finn, and he turned to the second man. 'What thing can you do best in all the world?'

'I am a tracker,' said the man. 'I can track the wild-duck over the nine waves in nine days.'

'And you?' said Finn to the third man. 'What thing can you do best?'

'I am a gripper. When I grip I never let go until my arms tear their roots out of my shoulders as the thing I have in my grip comes to me.'

'And what is your skill?' said Finn to the fourth man.

'I am a climber. I can climb a single thread of silk whose other end is fastened to the third star of Orion's Belt.'

'And yours?' said Finn to the fifth man.

'I am a thief. I can steal a heron's egg from the nest while the mother bird stands by and watches.'

'And yours?' said Finn to the sixth man.

'I am a listener. I can hear what people whisper to each other, lip to ear, at the other end of the world.'

'And yours?' said Finn Mac Cool to the seventh man, the last man of all.

'I am a marksman. I can pierce an egg thrown into the sky as far as the strongest bow can send an arrow.'

'Then indeed you can be of service to me,' said Finn Mac Cool, and gave each man his orders.

So the Shipwright felled the alder tree and cut it into planks and built a ship, with three blows of his axe. And they ran it down into the shallows, and Finn took the steering oar, for that was always the place of the leader. And the Tracker went and stood in the bow to guide them in the wake of the other vessel that nobody else could see or smell. And the rest pulled at the oars, and helped by the square sail they sped through the water with the speed of one of Manannan the Sea God's white-maned horses.

And at sunset they came to land.

They ran their ship up on to the shingle, where the stranger-chief's war-boat already lay at rest, and made towards the place, far up the glen that opened to that part of the shore, where they could see hearth smoke rising among the hazel and alder woods.

They came to a fine house in a clearing, with a level green all about it, and out strode the Young Hero to greet them, and flung his arms about Finn's shoulders.

'So you are come!'

'I was hungry and thirsty, also presently I shall wish to sleep,' said Finn, with the laughter hooking up the corners of his mouth.

'Eat and drink now,' said the Young Hero. 'Sleep must wait a while.'

And with his arm still across Finn's shoulders, he led them into his hall, and sat them down to the noble supper which his people brought in on chargers as broad as so many war shields and set before them. And while they ate roast boar and salmon, and drank heather-tasting yellow mead, he told Finn why he had brought him there.

'Seven years ago, I paid the bride-price for a maiden who my heart sang to, and brought her home from her father's hearth to mine. A year later to the day, she bore me a son, and I thought myself the most happy man on earth, until that same night a great hand came down through the chimney-hole, and snatched the babe from his mother's side. Three years ago this very night, my wife bore me another son, but again the hand came down through the chimney-hole, a great black hand gnarled like a tree root, and snatched that babe from us also. And now tonight my wife lies in the women's quarters, with her time come to bear a third. That is the reason that I came seeking your aid, and laid you under geise to follow me before you should eat or drink or sleep.'

'This is an ill story,' said Finn, 'but if it can be done, I and my men will surely save the third babe for you. Take me now to the women's quarters, and let my men sleep close outside.'

So the Young Hero led them to the women's quarters behind the hall, where his wife lay under a coverlid

of fine embroidered crimson cloth, with all the women
of the household busy about her.

And Finn went in and sat himself down by the hearth
to watch, while his men lay close outside. And
whenever he felt sleep drawing near, he drove his
hand against the sharp edge of the iron bar from which
the cauldron hung, and so kept wakeful with his wits
about him.

At midnight the child was born, and hardly had the
women helpers cried out that it was a son, than a great
black hand, gnarled as a tree root, came down through
the chimney-hole, and reached out to snatch the tiny
squalling thing.

Then Finn called to the Gripper, and the Gripper
seized hold of the hand and wrestled with it. He was
shaken to and fro as a rat is shaken by a dog, but his
grip never slackened, until a howl of rage and agony
burst upon them from overhead, and down through the
chimney-hole crashed the great black arm, torn out by
the roots from its owner's shoulder. But quick as the
strike of a snake, the other hand came down after it
and snatched up the babe and was gone.

Grief and wailing rose in the Young Hero's house,
and all his people looked at Finn as men look on one
who has failed them.

Then Finn swore a great oath. 'Before dawn myself
and my men will be on the trail of this hand, and if
we do not bring your son safe back to you, may none
of us ever return to our own hearths again!'

They went down to the shore once more, and ran
their ship down into the shallows and sprang on board.
And once again Finn went to the stern and took the
steering oar, and the Tracker went to the bow and

stood there sniffing like a hound, and said, 'This way, and no other, the track runs through the water.'

And Finn steered as the Tracker bade him.

All that day they followed the wave-trail as the Tracker sniffed it out, and just at sunset they saw far ahead of them a dark speck on the water that was too small for an island and too large for a gull. As they drew nearer, they saw by the last rays of the sun and the first rays of the moon that it was a tower rising sheer out of the water, and the roof of it shining darkly silver over all.

They rowed towards it until the galley touched against the walls. Then while the others rested on their oars, the Climber set one foot on the gunwale and the other on the wall of the tower, and walked up it as though he had been a fly.

In a while he came back, and dropped into the waiting boat.

'Well?' said Finn.

'Well enough,' said the Climber. 'The roof of this tower is made of eelskins on which a man must be slipping and sliding at every step. Otherwise I had been back sooner.'

'You are back now,' said Finn. 'What word do you bring with you?'

'I reached the smoke-hole in the crest of the roof, and looked down through it, and below me I saw the giant lying on his bed with a silk coverlid over him and a satin sheet under him, his left shoulder swathed in bloody linen, but the babe asleep in his outstretched right hand. On the floor of the chamber two young boys were playing shinty with golden sticks and a silver ball, and beside the hearth a wolfhound bitch lay suckling two pups, one grey and one brindled.'

'Well, indeed,' said Finn. 'Now it is the turn of the Thief. But you must go up again, carrying him on your back, for no one save yourself could climb these sheer walls and a roof as slippery as moonshine.'

So the Climber went up again, carrying the Thief on his back, and it was more than once they went, and brought away everything that was in the chamber; the boys with their golden shiny sticks and silver ball, the wolfhound pups from their mother's flank, the silk coverlid and even the satin sheet on which the giant lay and the new-born babe from the hollow of his right hand. Everything except the wolfhound bitch and the giant still sleeping on his stripped bed.

Finn wrapped the babe in the coverlid, and laid him in the hollow of the ship, with the hound pups on either side for warmth; and the rowers bent to their oars; and so they drew off from the giant's tower, making all speed on their homeward way.

Now the Listener had stationed himself in the stern, beside Finn at the steering oar, and they had not gone far when he said, 'I hear the gaint waking, for he is cold without his bedclothes. He is looking for the babe and the other things, but chiefly he is looking for the babe; and he is angry. He is very angry. Now he is sending the wolfhound after us. Row as hard as ever you can, for she too is angry!'

The rowers bent to their oars with redoubled effort, and the ship leapt through the water like a sea-swallow that outruns the waves, but before long they saw the wolfhound coming after them, swimming so fast that

red sparks sprang from her muzzle and flanks, and
streamed away in her wake.

'If she so much as brushes alongside us she'll set the
planking alight,' said Finn. 'Throw out one of the
pups, and maybe she will be turning aside to save the
creature and take it back.'

So they flung overboard the grey pup, and sure
enough the mother lost all interest in the boat, and
seizing the floundering puppy by the scruff of its neck,
she turned about and swam back the way she had
come, growing smaller and smaller until she disappeared into the distance and the first light of morning.

Finn's men rowed till their hearts were like to burst,
but after a while the Listener, standing beside Finn in
the stern, said, 'The hound bitch has got back to the
tower. The giant is very angry. He is ordering her to
come after us again; I can hear how he rages at her,
but she will not come; she will not leave the pup she
saved. She is telling him so, as a hound speaks with
its ears laid back and teeth bare. Now he has given up
trying to send her. And now — now he is coming after
us himself!'

'Row as you never rowed before!' said Finn. And
the rowers sent the ship whistling over the wavetops
more swiftly than the west wind itself, but before long
they saw the giant coming, and the western waters
reaching only midway up his thighs, and the waves
boiling into whirlpools all about him at every step. On
he came, striding in their wake, and for all their
desperate struggling at the oars, his stride brought him
closer and closer yet.

Then Finn put his thumb between his teeth, the
thumb which he had burned when he was cooking

Fintan the Salmon of Knowledge, and instantly it came to him that the giant was charmed against all weapon wounds save in one place, and that place a mole on the palm of his one remaining hand. And only through the mole could he be slain.

Finn told the Marksman this, and Marksman said, 'If I can catch but a single glimpse of that mole, he is a dead giant.'

Then the giant reached the stern of the ship, and towering over it like a crag, he reached out to grasp the masthead.

As he opened his hand to do so, the mole on the palm of it showed for one instant, and in that instant the Marksman notched an arrow to his bow, and drew and loosed. The arrow sped true to its mark, and with a yell that echoed from the sea to the sky and back again the giant fell dead.

The crash of his fall was like a mountain falling into the sea, and the ship rocked wildly, plunging under them like a startled horse, then righted itself and rode clear.

'That was a near thing,' said Finn, 'and that was a fine shot. Now we will be turning about and heading back to the giant's tower, for it is not in my mind to leave a good hound or a strong pup masterless in such a place.'

So they brought the ship about, and they rowed and sailed back to the giant's tower, and took the grey pup again, and with him his dam, who seemed now to be no more savage than any other hunting dog. And then for the last time they pulled away from the tower and set the galley's head toward the Young Hero's landing-beach and the Glen of the Hazel Woods. They rowed more slowly now, for they were very weary and there was no longer any pursuit to fear, and it was dawn of the next day when they came to the landing-beach.

They ran the boat up the shingle to its place beside the Young Hero's galley, and went on up the glen towards the house, Finn walking ahead with the babe still wrapped in the silken coverlid, the strange crew following with the other two boys, the hound bitch and her puppies, the satin sheet and the golden shinty sticks and the silver ball.

The Young Hero saw them at a distance and came to meet them. And when he saw not only the babe tucked under Finn's arm, but the two boys, he wept for the joy of finding all his sons again, when he had hoped only for the return of the last born. He knelt to Finn as though he were Cormac the High King, and begged to know what would seem to the Fian Captain a fitting reward, for all that he owned was Finn's for the asking.

'Give me my choice of the two hound pups,' said Finn, 'for truly I never saw any that showed better promise.'

Then they all went into the Young Hero's hall, where a great feast was made ready for them. And they remained with the Young Hero for a year and a day, hunting or trying their prowess at shinty and in all manner of sports and pastimes by day, and feasting royally by night. And if the last night's feasting was not the best of all, it was assuredly not the worst, even though the shadow of parting lay over it.

And when they sailed for Erin the next day, Finn took with him the brindled and white-breasted hound, now full grown, while the dam and the other yearling remained with the Young Hero who had named him Skolawn, which means Grey Dog.

Finn called the brindled hound Bran, and he was the first of his two favourite hunting dogs.

5
Finn and the Grey Dog

The months went by and the months went by, and again Finn and his companions went hunting. They had made their kill and were on the point of turning home by Almu of the White Walls when a stranger came to them.

This was a tall youth with hair as barley-pale as Finn's own, and eyes the colour of winter seas. 'You will be Finn Mac Cool, Captain of the Fianna of Erin?' said he, singling out Finn from his fellows, as most people could do easily enough by his great height and his air of having the very sun at his feet for a shinty ball.

'I am so,' said Finn, 'and who are you? And where from? And what bring's you seeking Finn Mac Cool?'

'As to the first, my name would mean nothing to you,' said the boy. 'As to the second, I am from the East and from the West; your name is known in both places. As to the third, I am wanting a master to serve for a year and a day.'

'And if I take you into my service, what reward will you demand at the end of the year and a day.'

'Only that you come and feast with me in the royal palace at Lochlan,' said the boy.

Now Lochlan was the homeland of the Vikings, the sea raiders, and the chief war-task of the Fianna was to keep the coasts of Erin safe from their raids and harryings. So Finn knew that this bidding to feast in the royal palace of Lochlan was like to be a trap. But there was always the chance that it was a holding out of the hand of friendship, and if that were so, a sore thing it would be to refuse. And Finn was never one to turn from a thing just because it smelled of danger. So he said, 'That seems a small enough wage. Serve me well, and I will pay it gladly.'

So the boy became one of Finn's household, and served him faithfully for a year and a day. And at the end of that time he came to Finn on the level green before the walls of Almu. 'The year is finished and the day is finished. Have I served you well?'

'You have indeed,' said Finn.

'Then now I claim my wages. Come with me to the royal palace of Lochlan.'

'Surely I will come,' said Finn, but to his own men he said, 'Fian Brothers, if I am not back among you within a year and a day, whet your spears and furbish your war-bows to avenge me on the shores of Lochlan.'

Then he went into the house-place to make ready for the journey. His druth, his jester, sat by the fire, and the tears ran down his long crooked nose and hissed as they fell into the hot ashes. 'Ach now, a fine sort of jester you are,' said Finn, thumping him lightly on the shoulder in passing. 'You should be making some fine jest to cheer me on my journey.'

'It is not I that am feeling like making jests,' said the little man, rubbing his shoulder.

'Are you sorry that I am going to Lochlan?'

'I am sorry. But though I cannot think of a jest to make you laugh at the outset of your journey, I can give you a piece of good advice to carry if you can find room for it.'

'And what is that?' said Finn.

'Take with you Bran's golden chain.'

'That seems very strange advice, but I will take it,' said Finn. And so when he set out, following the Lochlan boy, Bran's golden chain was bound like a rich belt about his waist. The Lochlan boy led the way, and so swiftly did he cover the ground that for all Finn's long legs, the Fian Captain could never overtake him, nor even come nearer to him than to see him always just disappearing over the next hill. So it was when he came to the coast, to a sheltered bay that he never remembered having seen before, and found a Lochlan galley waiting for him. The boy had gone ahead in another galley and was already far out to sea.

For many days they sailed and rowed until they came to the shores of Lochlan, and then to the royal palace. And when Finn reached the forecourt with the crew of the ship that had brought him there all about him, the boy was already sitting at the High Table in the King's hall, with the King his father. The King's hall was fine and proud to see, both inside and out. Gilded stags' horns crowned the roof that towered above the lesser roofs of the palace, and within the walls were hung with fine stuffs to keep out the draughts, and enriched with gold and enamel and walrus ivory, the harvest of many raids. Long tables of polished wood, already crowded with the sea-warriors and their women, were loaded with food and drink for a feast.

Finn entered the hall, still with the galley's crew about him. And since no one came to him with the guest cup, nor bade him come up to the High Table, he sat himself quietly down on a bench among them, and looked about him warily, and waited for what might happen next.

At the High Table the Lochlan lords had gathered together. They spoke low-voiced among themselves, glancing often in the direction of Finn. And Finn did not need to put his thumb between his teeth to know that whatever they said, it boded no good to himself. And he thought. 'So I have indeed walked into a trap. And now I must get out of it as best I may.'

But the door was shut behind him, and the galley's crew ringed him round.

'Hang him,' said one noble.

'Ach no,' said another. 'We should have to get a rope and bring it in, while all the while, here is the hearth fire all ready to our hands. Let us burn him and be done with it.'

'Die he must,' said a third, an old man with skin burned by sun and spindrift and eyes narrowed by gazing into the distances of many seas, 'but let it be by water; drowning is a death for a man.'

And at that moment there rose far off a mournful sound that might have been the cry of a wolf or the howl of a savage and despairing dog. And the Viking lords looked at each other and smiled in their yellow beards.

'Grey Dog shall do the killing for us.'

'And most willingly, too.'

'Aye. It has been death to any man to go near him since we captured him in that raid on the Glen of the Hazel Woods and brought him to Lochlan. Let us just take the man Finn to Glen More and leave him there. Grey Dog will see to the rest.'

Then one of them made a signal to the seamen surrounding Finn and they caught his arms and twisted them behind him. And struggle as he would, he could not win free, for they were too many for him, though each one by himself he could have broken like a dead stick across his knee. So at last he ceased to struggle and stood quiet, saving himself for a later time.

And in the distance, the dog howled again.

'Now, take him to Glen More and leave him there,' said the King of Lochlan.

The young Prince said, 'I will come too. It was my year and a day of service that won him here from Erin.'

And he looked at Finn with pleasure, as a hunter looks at his kill which other men have hunted in vain.

And the lords of the High Table looked at each other with savage and silent laughter.

In the distance, the dog howled a third time.

Finn heard it, and his belly knotted itself up small under his breastbone. But he thought, 'If I start my fight here, with the door shut, and all these men about me, then I shall be a worse fool than I was for coming here in the first place. Maybe somewhere between here and Glen More I will be getting my chance.'

So he stood unresisting while they bound his wrists, only he tightened all his muscles and made his wrists as thick as might be, so that when he let go, the bonds were slacker than the men who had bound him could possibly have guessed. And as they began to thrust him towards the door, he shouted up to the High Table, 'If this is Lochlan faith and Lochlan hospitality, then give me the faith and hospitality of wolves, which is altogether a truer and a kindlier thing!'

Then someone cursed, and struck him across the mouth, and he was hustled out through the door, which some of them ran to unbar, and away over the hills in the evening light, with never a chance to break out from among them, until they came to Glen More.

Glen More was a narrow gash among the hills, walled on either side by sheer rock and scree which there could be no climbing. And somewhere ahead of them the unearthly howling of Grey Dog echoed back from the rocks; a sound to make the bravest man's hair rise on the back of his neck. In the mouth of the Glen they passed a tiny bothie where an old man and wife lived, whose daily task was to feed Grey Dog. But even they did not dare to approach the terrible creature, and only went each morning to a certain hazel tree beside the burn, and flung the lumps of raw meat as far as they could up the Glen from there, and then ran back and barricaded the door of the bothie until the sounds of snarling and worrying told them that Grey Dog had come for his food, and the silence afterwards told them that he had gone back again into the further fastnesses of the Glen.

The men in charge of Finn urged him on, past the hazel tree, to the place where blood and bits of splintered bone showed where Grey Dog had devoured the whole of a buck flung out for him that day. But his howls that now seemed to echo all about them had not the sound of a creature full-fed and contented, but rather of a lost soul in torment and savage with hate of all the world.

'And this is far enough for us to be going,' said one

of the men, *I've* no mind to go the way of today's fat buck.'

'Nor I,' said another. 'The sooner and the further we are away from here the happier I shall be.'

'A pity it is that we cannot be staying a while to watch,' said the prince regretfully.

'Neither you nor us,' said the first. 'You would be welcome to stay and watch alone — it is not us that would be spoiling your pleasures, my young fighting-cock — but the King your father might not be best pleased to lose his son, and it is us that would suffer for it.'

Then Finn heard running feet behind him, growing smaller into the distance, and knew that he was alone, with his hands bound, and the wind blowing up the Glen, so that it must carry his scent to Grey Dog.

'Well,' he said to himself, 'there's no climbing out of this place. If I run, the men will kill me, and if, as it seems, I am to die anyway, I had sooner die from the fangs of this Grey Dog than at the hands of the Lochlan men. But the first thing is to get my own hands free.'

And he made his hands as narrow as might be, and pulled and strained and twisted until the veins of his forehead stood out, and the red blood sprang from his galled wrists, and at last he dragged his hands free, and dropped the binding-thongs to the ground behind him. And there he stood and waited for the next thing. And then far up from the Glen he heard Grey Dog coming, and soon he broke from cover into sight. Then Finn wondered if it would not have been better to run after the Lochlan men and die fighting them with his naked hands, after all. Grey Dog himself seemed no more than a shadow padding down between the rocks, and a snarling and a baying that grew louder every moment, but the breath that came from his snarling muzzle was a flame of fire that scorched and shrivelled everything in his path.

The blast of it caught Finn while the hound was still afar off, and his skin reddened and blistered and cracked. But he stood his ground, and suddenly he remembered the words of the jester, beside the hearth fire at Almu of the White Walls. 'Take Bran's golden chain with you,' and he knew what he must do.

He waited unitl Grey Dog was close upon him and he could bear the fiery breath no longer; and then he tore the golden chain, already glowing red-hot, from about his waist and shook it towards Grey Dog, as a man shakes the leash towards his hunting dog when he wants him for the chase, or the bridle towards his horse when he wishes him to come to the chariot yoke.

Grey Dog stopped in his tracks, and the fire of his breath sank low. Finn shook the chain a second time, and Grey Dog crouched on his belly, his muzzle in his paws while the flame of his breath died quite away. Finn shook the chain a third time, and Grey Dog cocked his ears, then sprang up and came with his tail waving behind him, to lick Finn's burns with a gentle tongue so healing that the pain went out of them on the instant. Then Finn stooped and fondled his ears as he might have done Bran's, and Grey Dog rubbed and butted his head against Finn's knees. And while he did so, Finn put Bran's golden chain round his neck and said, 'Come then, Skolawn.'

And they went down the Glen together.

As they came towards the bothie at the Glen foot, the old woman, who was standing in the doorway, ran in to her husband by the hearth.

'Husband! Husband! I have just seen such a sight as I never thought to see!'

'And what sight was that, then?' asked the old man, not even troubling himself to look up from the straw that he was braiding into a new ox collar.

'I have seen the man again, the man who the King's warriors were thrusting in their midst when they passed this way a while and a while back. The tallest and best-to-look-at man that ever I saw; the hair of him like barley under a white sun-haze, and the eyes of him grey as a gull's wing; and him coming down the Glen with Grey Dog on a golden chain pacing at his heels as quiet and friendly as our old Lop-Ear herself!'

Then the husband abandoned his ox collar and scrambled to his feet. 'That must be Finn Mac Cool, for of all the men of Lochlan and of Erin, only Finn could tame Grey Dog, and with Bran's golden chain to help him.'

So they went out of the bothie to meet Finn as he came down the Glen with Skolawn pacing at his heels.

Finn greeted them and told them of all that had happened, and asked for a meal and a place to lie down and rest, hidden from his enemies.

'As to yourself, you are most welcome to enter, and to share our fire and all that we have, even for a year and a day,' said the old man, 'but as for the dog — Grey Dog . . .'

'His name is Skolawn,' Finn said, 'and he will be no more trouble nor danger to you than any other hound entering your houseplace at his master's heels.'

So Finn entered, and Skolawn behind him, and there they remained for a year and a day with the old man and his wife; and none of the Lochlan nobles knowing that Finn was not dead, but lying hid there.

At the end of the year and a day, the old woman was standing on the hillock close by her houseplace. And looking towards the sea, she saw a thing that sent her screeching back to the bothie like a hen with the eggs stolen from under her.

'There are stranger war-boats all along the strand, and a great army landing from them on the beach!'

'Who leads them?' said Finn, who was sitting by the hearth, helping the old man to mend a fishing net.

'A tall proud man with one eye. By the look of him I'd say he has no equal for fighting under the stars.'

'That will be Goll Mac Morna,' said Finn, 'and the fighting men he leads are mine, the Fianna of Erin. But do not be afraid, no harm shall come to you, for the year and a day that I have eaten your food and slept safe by your hearth.' And whistling Skolawn to heel, he strode out to meet his old companions.

They raised a great shout at sight of him, and came running up from the shore. But away ahead of them, travelling in long leaps and bounds with his plumed tail flying like a banner behind him, came his great hound Bran. Skolawn sprang forward snarling, then checked as the brindled one came up, and they walked round each other stiff-legged, their hackles stirring and half lifting on the backs of their necks. Then Bran gave a deep and joyful bark, and crouched on his front paws, stern in the air like a pup that wants to play, and next instant he and Skolawn were spinning in circles round each other, with yelpings and small excited whines — for they were litter brothers, though they had been parted from each other when they were so young that they still suckled at their mother's flank; and they were not as other hounds, but had each a man's heart in them, so that after the first few moments of their meeting they knew their brotherhood to each other.

Then both together they flung themselves joyfully upon Finn, leaping about him and rearing up to plant their forepaws on his shoulders, and lick his face, so that any ordinary man would have been flat on his back before they were finished.

But by then the men from the war-boats had come up, and there were greetings and rejoicings all round.

'Here we are come to avenge you, and you strolling down to meet us, strong and well as though you had feasted every night in your own hall!' shouted Goll, with his arm across Finn's mighty shoulders. But the joy of the Fianna turned to anger when Finn told them how he had been received in the King of Lochlan's palace, and swords were out on the instant, and the men swearing vengeance after all.

And the vegeance of the Fianna started at one end of Lochlan and did not end until it came to the other. Only the old man and woman in the bothie at the foot of Glen More suffered no harm.

And that was how Finn Mac Cool came by the second of his two favourite hunting dogs.

6
The Birth of Oisīn

Again, Finn and his companions rode hunting in their home woods, and as they returned at evening towards Almu of the White Walls, suddenly a young dappled hind sprang up from the fern and foxgloves of a little clearing, almost under the nose of Finn's horse, and bounded away into the trees.

Finn's companions set up a great burst of hunting cries, and slipped the hounds from leash, and the hounds, weary as they were, sprang away on the track of the fleeing hind, and instantly the whole hunt swept after them, all the weariness of the day forgotten in the music of the hounds and the rush of the horses' speed and the excitement of the new chase.

But Finn noticed a strange thing, that however much the hind doubled and twisted in her track, she was drawing steadily nearer to the Hill of Almu itself. Almost it seemed as though she were trying to reach the place, like one running for sanctuary, yet what sanctuary could a hunted hind look for in the dun of the hunter?

On they sped, the hind well ahead, seen and lost among the trees, the hounds streaking on her trail, the horsemen thundering after. But the hind was as swift as the cloud shadow on a March day, and soon only Finn himself and his two great hounds still had her in sight, while the rest of the hunt fell farther behind, and at last all sound of them was lost in the wind-rustle and bee-drone and cuckoo-call of the summer woods.

Once the hind checked her speed and glanced back, as though to see who rode close on her trail, then fled on again, with Bran and Skolawn close behind her.

For a few moments the three were lost to view, where the alder and hazel and quicken trees clustered thick along the fringes of the forest, and then, as he crashed out through the undergrowth on to the open moors that surrounded the Hill of Almu, Finn came upon the strangest sight that ever he had seen. For

there in a little hollow set about with fern and shadowy with harebells, the hind lay panting from her long run, and Bran and Skolawn were standing over her, licking her face and her trembling limbs as though to tell her that she was safe with them and had nothing now to fear.

And while Finn stood staring, and the hind turned her graceful head and looked at him with the soft long-lashed eyes of her tribe, he heard the Fian hunting horn, and then the music of the hounds close at hand.

The hind sprang to her feet and stood trembling, and instantly Bran and Skolawn set themselves on either side of her, their hackles rising as they prepared if need be to fight. Then Finn wheeled his horse across the path of the hunt as they came up, and shouted to the Fianna to call off their hounds.

The horsemen reined in, pulling the horses back on their haunches, and seeing what was behind their Captain, called off their hounds in a hurry, for they knew Bran and Skolawn when their hackles rose like that, and knew that any hound who took up their challenge would be a hound lost to the pack. But Goll Mac Morna looked at the trembling hind and said, 'This is surely a strange quarry that you have run to bay.'

'It is in my mind that she was striving to reach Almu,' Finn said, half laughing at the foolishness of his own thought, yet holding to it all the same, 'and a poor thing it would be if a man were to hunt the guest who seeks his gates.'

So the hunting party rode on, across the level country and up the Hill of Almu. And sure enough, the hind went ahead of them, and she playing with Bran and Skolawn by the way. And when they came to the gates, in she went, and that evening at supper she lay at Finn's feet, with the two great hounds one on either side of her.

In the midst of that night, Finn woke with a start. His sleeping hut was white with moonlight that flooded in through the open door, and standing in the heart of the moonlight, like the gold in the heart of a white flower, was the most beautiful maiden that ever his eyes had touched upon. She wore a gown of soft saffron wool clasped at the shoulder with yellow gold, and out of it her neck rose white, and her slim bare arms were white, and her hair was so warmly golden that even the moon could not wash the gold out of it. Only her eyes were soft and dark and shadowed with long black lashes as the eyes of the hind had been.

'Who are you?' said Finn, wonderingly, and came to his elbow under the silken coverlid, 'and what is it that you do here? For you are no woman of Almu that I have ever seen before.'

'If you wish for a name to call me by, then call me Saba,' said the maiden. 'I am the hind that you hunted today.'

'This is beyond my understanding,' said Finn, rubbing his hand across his forehead. 'Am I dreaming? If so, I hope its a dream I'll be remembering in the morning.'

'You are not dreaming,' the maiden said. 'Listen, and you shall understand. Three of your mortal years ago, the Dark Druid of my own people tried to force his love on me and have me for his wife, and because I would have none of him, he used his magic to put upon me the hind's shape that I have worn ever since. But a slave of his who took pity on me and had good cause to hate him, told me that if I could win to the Dun of Almu, within the white walls of Finn Mac Cool, I should be safe from the spells of our dark master, and my true shape would come to me again. But for long and long, I could not come close to the

Dun, for fear of your dogs and your hunters, until today I found the chance to let myself be run down by you and no other hunter, and by your dogs Bran and Skolawn, who have enchantment in them also, and the hearts of men, and who would know me for what I am and do me no harm.'

'Here you are safe indeed,' Finn said, 'and none shall harm you or seek to force his love on you nor bind you with any bond against your will. But can you be happy among mortal folk, and you with never one of your kind to speak with or to touch your hand?'

For he knew that her own people of whom she spoke were the Danann People, the Proud Ones, the Fairy Kind.

'I will tell you that at another time. Now it is enough to be safe,' said Saba, and she smiled a little, and turned and went out of the sleeping hut. And as she went, she seemed to take the whiteness of the moonlight with her.

So Saba remained in the Dun of Almu. And Finn grew to love her, until the day came when he asked her to drink the bride-cup with him. And he did not ask lightly, for well he knew the sorrows and hazards that might be in store for a mortal man who takes a bride from the Fairy Kind.

'You asked me once,' Saba said, 'if I could be happy among mortal folk, with none of my own kind to speak with or to touch my hand.'

'And you said that you would tell me another time.'

And Saba said, 'I will tell you now. I can be happy anywhere in the Three Worlds with you, and not happy anywhere without you. You have done that to me, you who promised that in Almu no one should bind me with any bond against my will.'

So she became Finn's wife, and their happiness was like the happiness of the Immortals in the Land of Youth where spring never turns to winter, and magic birds sing always in the branches of the white apple trees whose blossom never falls, even when the apples sweeten and turn gold.

The months went by, and they wanted nothing in the world but to be in each other's company. Indeed, as moon followed moon, and summer turned to autumn and autumn to winter and back to spring, and Finn seemed to have no taste left for war or hunting or anything that could take him from her side, the Fianna began to mutter among themselves that their Captain was not the man he had been before her coming.

And then one day word came to Almu of the White Walls that there were Lochlan war-boats in Dublin Bay.

Then Finn roused himself, and called out the Fianna of the Five Provinces. And in the forecourt of Almu, as in other strongholds through the length and breadth of Erin, the warriors gathered to sharpen sword and spear blade on tall weapon stone.

Saba seemed to grow whiter and thinner as she watched, and once she said to Finn with her arms round his neck, 'Need you go?'

'A bargain is a bargain, and payment must be earned,' Finn said. 'The men of Erin pay us tribute and give us the shelter of their hearths and the food from their store sheds, that we may keep the shores of Erin for them, from the menace of the sea raiders. And shall we take the tribute, and eat from the store sheds and warm ourselves at the hearths, and not keep the shore in return?'

'But need *you* go?' said Saba.

And Finn thought, 'That is the Fairy Kind speaking,' but he said only, 'The Fianna of the Five Provinces do not go into battle without their leader.' And then he told her a thing that Goll Mac Morna had once said: 'A man lives after his life, but not after his honour,' and gently pulled her arms from about his neck, and went out to see how the armourers were doing.

At the very last, with the warriors waiting before the gates, he said, 'Wait for me, bride-of-my-heart, and soon we shall be together again. But while I am away, promise me that you will not set foot outside the walls of Almu, nor speak to anyone not of our household.'

And Saba promised, and Finn marched away at the head of the Leinster Fianna, towards the agreed hosting-place where the Munster and Mide, Connacht and Ulster battalions would join him.

Seven days they were fighting the sea raiders, and they drove them from the land and down the shore, and back, back, back to their ships — those that were left of them. But many a Lochlan man lay dead among the coast-wise hills of Erin, and many were left wounded or captive, to drag out their days with an iron slave collar round their necks herding cattle or threshing barley for an Irish master. And many a black war-boat staggered home with half her crew, or was left beached on the shores of Dublin Bay, for lack of enough men to work the oars. And these the Fianna fired, and left for so many beacons blazing along the shore behind them, when they turned home again on the eighth day.

With every step of the homeward way, Finn thought more strongly of Saba, and his heart went out ahead of him to be with her again. And when they reached the foot of the Hill of Almu and began to climb, his gaze went searching to and fro along the ramparts and among all the possible look-out places, for the first sight of her waiting for him. But no sign of Saba could he see. And when he came into the forecourt and looked about him, thinking that now surely she would come running, still there was no sign of her, not so much as the glimmer of a single golden hair. And his household hung back, with trouble in their faces, instead of crowding forward to greet him as they usually did, and seemed to find it hard to meet his eyes.

And suddenly a cold hand seemed to close on Finn's heart.

'Where is the Lady Saba?' he demanded. 'Is she sick? Why is she not here to greet me?'

Then his steward came forward with bent head, and told him what he asked.

'While you were away, Lord of Almu, aye, not three days since, we saw one coming up the hill towards the gate, who seemed in all things so far as the eye could tell to be yourself, and with him two hounds who had the outward seeming of Bran and Skolawn, even to the three black hairs on the tip of Skolawn's tail. And at the same time we seemed to hear the sound of the Fian hunting horn. Then the Lady Saba, who was watching from the gatehouse roof, as she had watched all and every day for your return, cried out glad and sweet, and hurried down to where the men were already opening the gate for your coming in. We shouted to her to remain within, but truly, it is in my mind that she never heard us, and she was out through the gate like the dart of a swallow, and running down the hill.'

'And then?' said Finn in a terrible voice.

'When she came close to him who wore your shape and seeming, she checked, and gave a loud, bitter cry, and turned to run back towards the gate. But he struck her with a hazel wand, and there, where she had been, was a dappled hind, and she doubling and twisting piteously as still she tried to reach the gate, and the two hounds drove her back. We seized our weapons and ran out to aid her, but when we reached the place, there was nothing to be seen. Neither hind nor hounds nor enchanter, not so much as their shadows on the bare hillside. And suddenly the air was filled with a great rushing, shouts and cries and hoof-drum of galloping horses and the baying of hounds, and some of us thought that it came from this direction and some that it came from that, until at last all died away into the wind. We have searched all the country round, but there is no trace of her nor of those who hunted her. Oh, my Lord Finn, the Lady Saba is lost to us!'

Then Finn covered his face with his hands, that no man might see the look on it, and went to his own chamber, speaking no word.

All that day and all the next, he remained shut away and no one dared to go near his door. And on the third day he came out, and took up his place and his duties as Captain of the Fianna once more.

Seven years went by before he rode hunting again, and all that time, whenever he was not with the High King nor on the war trail against the sea raiders, nor at the summer training, he went searching for Saba,

from North to South and from East to West. From
coast to coast of Erin he sought her, taking with him
no hounds but Bran and Skolawn, up every mountain
and down every glen and through the depths of every
forest and across the windy heights of every moor. But
nowhere did he find any trace of her.

And when the seven years were past, he gave up all
hope of finding her again, and began to hunt with the
rest of the Fianna as of old.

One day they were hunting on Ben Bulben in Sligo,
the hounds running far ahead, when he heard their
trail-music change to a fierce yelping and snarling like
a dog fight. He and his companions ran forward — they
were hunting on foot that day, for the mountain runs
were too steep for the ponies — and found a naked boy
standing under a quicken tree, the hounds striving to
seize him, all save Bran and Skolawn, who with fangs
bared and ears laid back, had sprung forward and
turned on the rest of the pack to hold them off.

Memory smote Finn under the heart, and he
remembered another time that he had come upon his
two great hounds doing this very thing. But then it had
been to protect a dappled hind . . .

His men gathered round, beating off the hounds,
while the boy stood quite unafraid, looking round
from one to another of them. He was tall and well
shaped, though slight of build — a runner rather than
a wrestler, thought Finn, who was used to judging in
these matters — and his hair was almost as pale as
Finn's own, so that his dark eyes seemed all the more
dark by contrast. He stood like a wild thing, tensed
and light on his feet, yet still proudly unafraid.

'Who are you?' Finn asked.

The boy looked at him, but spoke no word.

'What is your name? Where is it that you come from?'

Still the boy said no word, and suddenly Keelta Mac Ronan said, 'It is no good to ask him. Don't you see? He knows only the Wild. He does not understand man's tongue!'

So Finn held out his open hand to the boy, slowly and reassuringly, so that he might understand there was no menace in it. The boy looked from his face to his outstretched hand and back again. 'Come,' said Finn, as he might have said to a hound puppy he was training, knowing that the pup would not yet know the meaning of the word, but his voice speaking it would mean something all the same. And slowly, the boy came and set his hand in Finn's.

So they returned to Almu with the strange boy in their midst. And all the way, Finn watched him, as though some great questing was in his mind, and the boy was the answer.

At first he was like a wild creature caged. Everything was strange to him; clothes chafed and hampered him after running naked all his life, so he pulled off breeks and shirt again and again, and threw them away. He did not know how to eat among men, and would snatch his food and take it under the table with the hounds. But little by little he grew less wild; more used to the ways of men; he began to be able to guess what people meant when they spoke to him, though sometimes he guessed wrong, and brought Goll Mac Morna an apple when the old warrior had asked him to scratch the gad-fly bite between his shoulder blades, or came willingly to loose the thongs of Finn's hunting

shoes for him when the Fian Captain had only said that
the nights were growing colder. And at last, hesitating
and stumbling at the outset, he began to gain the power
of human speech.

And when speech came easily enough to him for
story telling, it was a strange story he had to tell Finn,
sitting between Bran and Skolawn at the Fian Captain's
feet, one winter's night with the wind howling like a
wolf pack about the door.

Ever since he could remember, he had lived with a
dappled hind. He supposed that she was his mother,
for he had had no other, nor any father, so far as he
knew. And she had given him milk when he was very
small, and the warmth of her body curled about him
when the nights were cold, and comfort when he was
hurt or unhappy, and love and gentleness at all times.
They had lived in a green and beautiful valley, from
which — he was not quite sure how or why — there
seemed no way out, but he supposed there must have
been, after all, because assuredly there was a way in,
though he had never found it. And this he knew,
because though he lived on nuts and berries in summer, in winter food was left for him daily in a certain
cave on the hillside; and also because a man came to
them at times, a very tall dark man, at whose coming
he had always been troubled and afraid. Sometimes
the man spoke to the hind his mother in tones that were
darkly sweet as heather honey, sometimes in a voice
hard with menace, but always the hind shrank away
and would not even look at him; until at last he went
off again, very angry.

And then there came a day when the dark stranger
spoke with his mother for a very long time, sometimes

pleadingly and gently, sometimes urgently and as though there were pain within him, sometimes ragingly, like a cold gale through the woods in winter, but still she would do nothing but shrink away from him, yet keeping always between him and the boy. At last the man gave up pleading and threatening alike, and did a thing that the boy had never seen him do before. He lifted up the hazel wand which he always carried in his hand and struck her with it, and then turned instantly and strode away.

And this time the hind followed him, trembling and seeming as though she strove to draw back, but following still.

Then the boy was terribly afraid, and cried out to his mother not to leave him. But when he would have run after her, his feet seemed to have taken root in the ground. And his mother looked back at him, piteously, the great tears falling from her eyes. Yet still she followed the dark man as though he drew her after him on a chain.

Then, still struggling to follow her, crying out in rage and terror and desolation, the boy fell to the ground, and into a blackness that was like sleep but not like good sleep.

When he awoke from the blackness, he was lying on the bare heather slopes of Ben Bulben. And he was alone.

For days he hung about the slopes of the mountain, seeking and seeking for his hidden valley, and never finding it again, until at last the Fian hunting dogs found him.

So Finn knew that he would never find Saba again, but he knew also that she had left him a son.

He called the boy Oisīn which means Little Fawn, and he grew up to become one of the greatest champions of the Fianna. But always there was a strangeness about him, for he was of the Fairy Kind on his mother's side. And famous warrior that he became, he was still more famous for the songs that he made and the strange and wonderful stories that he told, for from his mother's side he had the gift of minstrelsy, and he could sing a bird out of an arbutus tree or the morning star down from the skirts of the sunrise.

But the story of Saba and the Dark Druid he could not give an end to. No one knows the end of that story, to this day.

7

The Chase of Slieve Gallion

Cullen, the Smith of the Danann People, had his hall in the Fairy mound on Slieve Gallion near Armagh. And he had two daughters, one called Ainé and the other Milucra.

Beautiful they were, and like to each other as two white bramble flowers on a spray, and many fine tall warriors came seeking them in marriage. But both Ainé and Milucra had set their love on Finn Mac Cool, and would not so much as look at any other man. And both wanting the same man, they grew jealous of each other and were ready to do each other an ill turn at any hour of the day or night. But Finn Mac Cool was still searching for his lost love at that time, and had no eyes for either of them.

One day a chieftain came seeking Ainé for his wife. A fine tall man he was, with eyes as darkly blue as the hills of Connemara before rain and a neck as strong as a stallion's; but he was no longer young. Cullen thought well of the match. 'If you marry him, though to be sure he is mortal, and not of our blood, you will have a position that will bring on you the envy of half the women in Erin. Be thinking, my daughter, before you send him away as you have sent others.'

'I am not needing to think,' said Ainé. 'I am beautiful am I not? I can have mortal men with heads as black as a rook's wing or as yellow as birch leaves in autumn, or as red as a chestnut horse's coat. Or I can have men of our own Danann kind who will never grow old at all. Why then should I marry a man whose hair is already grey? Father, I will not do such a thing! Not until Lough Lein runs dry and Slieve Gallion falls into the sea!'

Now Milucra overheard this, and she thought to herself that if she could not get Finn Mac Cool for her own, (and she had begun to understand that she could not) here was a chance to make sure that her sister Ainé should not have him either. There would be some comfort in that, thought she. And she gathered together all those of her friends who were not also friends of

her sister's, and bade them come with her up to the little grey lough on the crest of Slieve Gallion. And there, forming a ring about the lough they loosed their hair and linked hands, and going round and about and against the wind and against the sun, they made a dancing magic that charged the water with a strong enchantment.

And long after this, Bran and Skolawn started a hind near the Hill of Almu, and ran it northwards towards Slieve Gallion. Finn followed, desperate for a closer view of the hind, though something deep within him told him that it was not Saba. But on the high mountainside she vanished as though the dark rocks had opened and let her through. And though Finn searched and searched, refusing to listen to the thing within him that knew the hind was not Saba, he could find no more trace of her than if she had been the end of a fading rainbow.

But in his searching he came upon the little lonely grey lough on the crest of the moutain. And there on the bank was a beautiful woman sitting with her head lowered on her knee, and weeping sore.

He drew closer, and asked her what terrible thing had happened to cause her so much grief.

'I have lost the gold ring that I prize most in all the world, for it was set on my finger by my young hero before he died. Now it has slipped off into the cold cruel water, and I shall never see it again.'

'I will get it back for you,' said Finn, and stripping off his hunting leathers he dived into the lough.

The water was cold as the green mountain spate that comes down in spring from the melting snows, and he went down and down into the strange twilight world at the heart of the lough. Jagged rocks loomed faintly through the dimness, and long green weed floated out towards him as though to entangle him and draw him into itself, but nowhere could he see any gleam of gold before he had to come up for air. The woman cried out to him from the bank, 'Try again! Oh, try again!' and again he dived, but with no more success than he had had the first time. And when he broke surface empty-handed, the woman cried to him, 'Try again! Oh, try again!' A third time he dived, and this time, lodged in a cranny between two boulders, he saw the glint of a golden ring. He snatched it up, and with his heart almost bursting through his ribs, kicked upward and rose to the surface of the water.

'I have it,' he shouted and struck out towards where the woman still sat on the bank.

'Give it to me!' she cried, so eager that it seemed she could not even wait for him to land, but leaned foward to take the ring he held out to her before his feet touched the bottom. But the instant she had it in her hand, she gave a strange high laugh, and dived into the water, making no more splash than an otter makes, and was gone.

Then Finn knew that some kind of magic was being worked against him, and the sooner he was out of the water and away from that place the better for him. He sprang ashore, but as he touched dry land, the clear mountain light dimmed as though a shadow had been drawn across his eyes, and his legs gave under him with a strange trembling weakness, and he ptiched forward on to his face. Slowly he contrived to prop himself up on his arms, and looked down with his strangely shadowed sight at his hands outspread on the turf among the little mountain flowers, and they were the knotted and thick-veined hands of an old, old man.

Cold horror seized on Finn, and he struggled to cry

out to Bran and Skolawn who were sniffing in a troubled way about the edge of the lough, but his voice came as a cracked whisper, and Skolawn only looked up for an instant and growled softly, as though warning the stranger to take no liberties, while Bran never turned for an instant from his desperate questing around the margin of the water. So even his own hounds did not know him.

Finn put his Thumb of Knowledge between his teeth, wondering if even that power was lost to him. But the power remained, and instantly he knew that Milucra the daughter of Cullen had been both the hind and the woman by the lough shore, he knew that all this was her doing, and he knew why she had done it.

Meanwhile, in Almu of the White Walls, the day wore on to supper time, and Finn had not returned, though there were guests at the hearth and all men knew that he would never be so lacking in courtesy as to leave them to sup without their host. Then Keelta Mac Ronan, he who could outrun the west wind, called for the swiftest runners among Finn's household, and with a couple of their best trail-hounds in leash, they set out to find him.

The hounds picked up his scent easily enough, and followed it without a check, and so just as the moon was getting up, they came to the little lonely lough on the crest of Slieve Gallion. And there on the lough shore they found a wretched, doddering old man, so weak that he could scarcely stand, and Bran and Skolawn questing to and fro among the grey rocks of the mountain top, who came to them whining in desperate trouble when they drew near.

'Old man,' said Keelta, 'has Finn Mac Cool passed this way?'

The old man stood wavering on his feet, and gazing from one to another strangely and terribly. They thought that he did not understand, perhaps age had made him wander in his wits. 'Finn Mac Cool,' they said, 'the Captain of the Fianna of Erin: have you seen him? You could not be mistaking him, a giant of a man with hair as pale as bleached barley.'

The old man seemed to be trying to answer, but his voice was no more than a wheezing mumble and they could not understand what he said.

At last he beckoned to Keelta, and when the swift-footed one stepped near, whispered to him with a great effort, 'I am Finn Mac Cool.'

Keelta started back, and stared wildly round at the others. 'The grandfather says — he says that *he* is Finn Mac Cool.'

The rest cried out in angry unbelief. 'The old man has taken leave of his wits! Or he seeks to play a trick on us! Throw him in the lough to learn better manners!' But Keelta saw something in the old man's face that made him bend close again.

And gathering himself for a mighty effort, for his remaining strength seemed ebbing moment by moment, Finn wheezed and gasped out the story of what had happened to him at the hands of Milucra, the daughter of Cullen the Smith.

Then the Fianna believed that the old man was indeed Finn, bound by Danann enchantment, and wrath seized them.

Keelta and another scrambled down the mountainside to where the trees began, and cut branches of

birch and quicken, and bringing them back, bound
them into the framework of a litter; they spread their
cloaks over the framework and lifted Finn into it.
Then, carrying him in their midst, they set out for the
Fairy mound where Cullen the Smith had his hall.

There they set down the litter, and with their broad
iron-bladed daggers, began to dig.

For three days and three nights they dug into the
Fairy mound, tunnelling deeper and deeper. And on
the third day they reached the innermost heart of it.
To their mortal eyes, their senses protected from the
Fairy glamour by the cold iron of the daggers with
which they dug, there was no splendid palace there,
no forecourt full of prancing horses, no banquet hall
brilliant with rich hangings and vessels of gold and
silver; only a dark earthen cavern, held up by rough
slabs of stone, but in the entrance to the cavern stood
Ainé, holding a great drinking cup of the reddest gold.

She smiled and said, 'That was good digging.'

'We had good cause,' said Keelta Mac Ronan.

'I was waiting for you,' said Ainé, still smiling, 'for
I know the magic of Milucra my sister, and I hold in
my hand that which shall undo the harm.' And she
went forward to the litter on which Finn lay, and held
out to him the golden cup.

He took it between his trembling hands and drank,
and instantly sprang from the litter, young and strong
and proud as ever he had been, only that his hair was
silver grey, as the seed silk of the willow herb.

'Drink again,' said she, 'and your hair also will be
as it was before.'

Finn half held out his hand, then drew it back. 'My
thanks to you that you have freed me from your sister's

spell-binding. But for the rest, I will keep my hair grey, Ainé; for I'm not minded to be husband of yours.'

Ainé snatched back the cup, and was gone, and nothing left but the grass-grown mound with a ragged hole in its side.

Then Finn and the Fianna whistled up their dogs and turned back towards Almu of the White Walls.

And Finn's hair continued silver to the end of his days.

8

The Giolla Dacker
and his Horse

The years went by and the years went by, and Finn
Mac Cool took a second wife, Manissa, daughter of
Garad of the Black Knee, and had other sons beside
Oisīn, but none that he loved so well. And he did not
hold back from his hunting to remain beside Manissa
as he had done to be always at Saba's side.

One summer Finn and the Fianna hunted the broad
runs of Munster. They hunted over Kenn-Aurat and
Slieve Keen and Coill-na-Drua, and across the rich
lands of Fermore, and south among the lakes of
Killarney; all the length of the great plain of Firmin
they hunted and up over the speckled crest of Slieve
Namon. All through East Munster and West Munster,
from Balla-Gavran to Limerick of the blue waters.

And while they were hunting the Plain of Cliach,
Finn caused the hunting camp to be pitched on the
level top of the hill that overlooked it, and went up
there himself to rest, and to watch the Fianna hunting
the lower ground. Several of his closest companions
were up there with him, among them Goll Mac Morna
of the Mighty Deeds, and Conan of the ram's fleece
and the bitter tongue, and Fergus Finvel his wisest
councillor, and Oisīn his own son, together with
Dearmid O'Dyna, both of them very young warriors,
new come to the Fianna.

When the Fian Captain and his companions had

taken their places on the hill, the hunters unleashed
their hounds and the summer morning grew full of the
sounds that Finn loved best to hear; the baying music
of the hounds and the cries and calls of the hunters
encouraging them on, and the notes of the hunting
horn echoing through the glens.

But presently, as he watched the movements of the
hunt, Finn saw coming up the hillside through the
woods that fleeced the lower slopes, a man leading a
horse. But surely the strangest and ugliest man leading
the strangest and ugliest horse that any of the watching
chiefs and champions had ever seen.

To begin with, both were of giant size, and the man
had a thick clumsy body set on bowed and twisted
legs, his feet broad and flat and his arms of gigantic
strength, his lips thick and his teeth crooked, and
himself the hairiest man that ever was seen. In his right
hand he held an iron-bound club which he dragged
behind him, and it tearing up the ground in a track as
broad as the furrow that a farmer ploughs behind a
team of oxen. And his horse — as they drew nearer,
Finn saw that it was an aged mare — was fit mount
for such a master. She was covered all over with a
tangle of rusty black hair as unkempt as an old furze
bush, her ribs and the knobbled ends of every bone
showed through her hide, her legs, like the man's,
were crooked, her neck twisted and her ugly head far
too big even for her enormous body. There was a
halter round her neck by which her master seemed to
be dragging her along by main force. Every now and
then the mare would dig in all four hooves and refuse
to move another step; then her master would bang her
in the ribs with the iron-bound club, and drag so hard

at the halter that it was a wonder her head didn't part company with her body. And every now and then she would give such a backward tug on the halter that it was as much of a wonder that the man's arm did not come out by the roots.

With all this pulling and hauling and jerking and banging, he could make but slow travelling, and it was a while before he reached the hill top where Finn and his companions stood watching. But when he did reach them, he bowed his head and bent his knee respectfully enough.

Finn asked him who he was and what he wanted, according to the usual custom.

'As to who I am, how should I know, for I never knew who my father and mother were either, but men call me the Giolla Dacker, the Hard Ghilli. As to what I want, Captain of the Fianna, I am a wanderer in many lands, selling my services to anyone who will pay and feed me. Often in my travels I have heard your name spoken, and your strength and wisdom and open-handedness praised, and therefore I am come to seek service with you for one year.'

'What wages do you ask?' said Finn.

'At the year's end, I will fix my own wages,' said the stranger.

'Will you so?' said Finn, amused at the giant's audacity.

'Aye, if you will have me. But first I must tell you that my name was not given me without good cause, for I am indeed a hard ghilli. Hard to move, hard to manage, hard to get along with. There never was a worse or lazier servant nor one that grumbled more at having to do the simplest job of work.'

'It's not a very pretty account that you give of yourself,' said Finn, 'but I never yet refused service and wages to any man who came seeking them, and I will not refuse you now.'

The Giolla Dacker grinned as though mightily pleased with himself, and took the halter off his miserable bony nag and turned her loose among the horses of Finn and his companions.

And then it appeared that the mare was even harder to get along with than her master, for no sooner was she among the other horses than she cocked her ugly head, stuck out her long rough tail stiff as a spear shaft behind her, and began to kick out at them in all directions. The Fianna ran, shouting, to put a stop to her ugly game, but she saw them coming, and with a shake of her head and a harsh defiant neigh, set off for the place close by where Conan Maol's horses were grazing by themselves.

Conan, seeing this, bellowed to the Hard Ghilli to catch his accursed horse before she could make any more mischief.

But for answer, the Hard Ghilli tossed him the halter, saying with a cavernous yawn, 'I'm tired. If you're wanting her fetched off from your precious beasts, go you and do it yourself.'

Conan in a spitting rage had no time to argue and use his familiar weapon of barbed words. He snatched up the halter and ran so fast that he came up with the ill-tempered mare just before she reached his horses, and flinging the halter over her head, tried to drag her round and lead her back to the others. But instantly the mare became as immovable as though she had turned into a tree and taken root. And though Conan hauled and heaved and tugged until he was purple in the face, he could not budge her one finger's breadth.

Meanwhile, the rest of Finn's companions who had followed, stood round holding their sides with laughter. Fergus Finvel said, snatching at his breath, 'I never thought to see our fat Conan playing horse boy to any man — and not over successfuly at that! Why are you not getting up on her back and showing her who's master, Conan Maol?'

Conan, stung by their jeers and laughter, scrambled on to the mare's back and began to kick her in the ribs and hammer his fists between her laid-back ears, to make her go. But the mare only drew back her lips as though she too were laughing, and remained immovable as ever.

'Och now, I know what the trouble is,' said Fergus Finvel. 'She has been used to the Giolla Dacker on her back, and him a giant no less, and fat as you are, like enough she cannot feel your weight, and is not even knowing she's a rider up there at all!'

'Well, that's a thing can be easily set right,' said Coil Croda the Battle-Victor, and he sprang up behind Conan. But still the mare never stirred. Then Dara Donn mounted behind Coil, and Angus Mac Airt behind *him*, and so on until there were fourteen of the Fianna sitting on the back of the Giolla Dacker's horse and belabouring her to make her move. And she not seeming to feel them there at all for the notice she took of them.

Then the Giolla Dacker flew into a great state of indignation, and turned on Finn shouting, 'I see now how much all these fine accounts of you are worth! Your men are pleased to make a mock of my horse and therefore of me, and you do nothing to stop them! I'll not stand it, I'm telling you! Pay me my money and let me go from your service!'

'That was a short service!' said Finn, bending over the laughter pain in his belly. 'The agreement was that you should claim your wages after a year.'

'On second thoughts,' said the Giolla Dacker, 'I'd not be accepting wages from such as you! And now I'm away to find a better master.'

And so saying, he turned and began to stroll slowly away in the direction of the coast of Kerry.

The mare seeing this, pricked up her lop ears and ambled quietly after him, the fourteen still on her

back, and the rest of the Fianna still doubled up with laughter to see them so. But before they had covered three times the length of their own morning shadows, the Giolla Dacker checked and looked back to make sure the horse was following him, then tucked up his kilt and went on again. But now he went with the speed of a swallow darting through the blue air, as a stone whirled from the sling; he went so fast that his bow legs were only a blur under him, and the mare neighed three times and quickened into a flying gallop to keep up with him. Now the fourteen on her back strove to fling themselves off, but they were held fast and could not tear themselves free.

Then their comrades, seeing that they were now really in trouble, stopped laughing, and gave chase all the way to the coast. When they reached the seashore they thought that surely the Giolla Dacker and his demon mare must stop, but he ran straight on out to sea, and the mare after him, plunging into the water without an instant's slackening of her speed. Ligan Lumina who could run almost as fast as Keelta Mac Ronan and jump further than any other man of the Fianna, had outdistanced the rest in the chase, and making one mighty leap, he actually caught the mare by the tail, just as she took to the water. But he might have had no more weight than a cockle-burr, for all the hindrance that he was to her, and as she plunged on through the shallows and into the deeps, towing him behind her, he found that his hands were stuck fast to her tail and he could no more let go than the fourteen riders could free themselves from her back.

Standing on the beach, spent and panting from their long and desperate chase, Finn and the rest saw their comrades carried out of sight. And wasting no time on exclaiming and lamenting, they set themselves to decide what was best to do. They determined to make for the coast below Ben Eader, where a ship was always kept fitted and ready for sea in case of need, and sail westward in search of their lost comrades. So Finn chose out fifteen of his best and bravest men to go with him, including old Goll Mac Morna and young Dearmid O'Dyna. But Oisín he left behind, because he was his eldest son and must captain the Fianna while he was away.

They set out for Ben Eader, and went on board the waiting ship, and sailed south and then west round the coast of Erin, then out into the bright western sea. They raised the square sail and the rowers bent to the oars, and the ship sped westward like a live and willing creature, until the green shores and the white sands of Erin were lost behind them.

Many days went by: and at last they saw ahead of them an island rising sheer out of the water as though to hit the clouds, and seemingly no way up the sheer cliffs at all.

They sailed and rowed right round the island, and still they found no way up, not so much as a mountain cat could climb. But they came to a place where Faltlaba, the best tracker among them, sniffed three times and said that both the Giolla Dacker and his horse had landed here. And since there was no sign of them at the foot of the cliff, it was clear that they must somehow have climbed it to the top.

Now all of them understood that at the back of these happenings there was enchantment of some kind, and that they had to do with the Lordly People, and of them all, the best fitted to go forward on an adventure of this kind was Dearmid O'Dyna, for he had been foster-reared in Brugh-Na-Boyna, by Angus Ōg himself, one of the greatest of the Danann Princes, though that is a story for telling at a later time.

So Dearmid rose in the ship, and put on his war gear, and slung his sword over his shoulder, and took his two long spears one in either hand, and the warrior's battle-fury came upon him so that the air glowed all about him and the clouds gathered over his head, and his beauty grew terrible to look upon. Then he crouched and made himself taut like a strung bow, and springing upward on the butts of his spears he made a great bound, and landed on a rock ledge far up the sheer face of the cliff. From there, using his spears and his hands and his feet, he leapt and swung from ledge to ledge and from cranny to cranny, working his way ever upward, while his comrades craned their necks to stare up at him from far and further below. And at last he gained the cliff top, and had green grass under his feet again.

Before him spread woods and thickets of fair and shady trees ringing with birdsong, and cool to the ear with the sound of running streams. And beyond the woods showed level grasslands gay with flowers of white and crimson and blue and yellow. Dearmid looked about him, and seeing still no sign of the Giolla Dacker or his horse, he thought that his best course was to walk straight on through the woods, for maybe in the open land on the far side he would find people who could tell him where to look for them.

So he left the cliff behind him and took to the trees, walking straight on, so far as he could judge his direction among their slender trunks and mazy branches, until at last he came out on the other side. And there ahead of him in the midst of a green meadow as smooth as a lawn, he saw a tall broad-headed apple tree heavy with fruit. Nine standing stones made a circle about it, and close beside it, in the centre of the circle, stood another stone, taller than all the rest. At the foot of this tallest stone, a spring of clear water bubbled up and flowed away in a looping stream across the meadow.

Dearmid was hot and thirsty after his climb, and he hurried towards the spring, and knelt to cup the water in his hands and drink. But as his lips touched the water he heard a low menacing murmur, the jink of weapons, the heavy tramp of feet, as though a whole war host were coming upon him across the plain. He let the water run back through his fingers, and starting up, looked about him. But the sounds had stopped on the instant, and there was nothing to be seen.

He stooped to drink again, and again came the sounds of an approaching war host. A second time Dearmid sprang up and looked all about him, and saw nothing, no one. But this time, chancing to glance up to the top of the pillar-stone, he saw lying there a beautiful speckled drinking horn, bound and rimmed with yellow gold and curiously enriched with jewels and coloured enamels.

'Maybe the well will not allow any man to drink its waters except from this horn,' thought Dearmid, and he reached up and took down the horn, dipped it into the water, and drank. This time he heard no sound of an advancing war host, but no sooner had he drained the last drop, then he saw coming towards him a tall man in a cloak of poppy red. A band of red gold held his dark hair back from from his forehead, and under it his face was dark with anger, so that he seemed altogther black-bloomed like a thunder cloud.

'Dearmid O'Dyna,' said the strange champion, 'is not Erin green and wide enough, and running with streams enough for your drinking, that you must come here into my broad green country, and take my drinking horn and drink from my well?'

'Surely this is a sorry welcome!' Dearmid said.

'You should not insult your host by making free with his hospitality if you want a better!' said the champion, and advanced on Dearmid with his sword out. Dearmid met him half-way, his own sword in his hand, and knee to knee, they fought like antler-locked stags in the autumn season.

All that day they fought, neither gaining any advantage over the other; all day till evening came. And as the sun was sinking, suddenly the champion sprang backward into the very centre of the pool and sank from sight, as though the spring had swallowed him.

Dearmid, very weary, stood on the brink, leaning on his sword and staring at the place where the champion had disappeared. Then (for he knew the ways of the Danann People), he spread his cloak under the apple tree, and lay down to sleep, until the champion of the spring, who had gone with the sun should come back with the sun again.

When he woke, the sun was just showing above the edge of the world, and already the champion of the spring stood ready beside the tall pillar-stone.

All that day they fought, as they had fought the day before, and at sunset, just as before, the champion sprang backward into the pool and sank from sight, and Dearmid spread his cloak under the apple tree and slept until sunrise. The third day it all happened just as before, and each morning the champion looked more darkly terrible than he had done the previous evening. But as the fourth day drew to a close, Dearmid was well prepared, and as the dark champion made his backward leap, the Fian warrior sprang forward and flung his arms round him so that they sank together.

Down and down they went, the light growing small like a green bubble overhead, into a darkness that was full of strange shifting shadows. Dearmid felt the shadows brushing against him though he could not see them, and it seemed to him that they had been sinking for long years of time and must go on sinking for ever, when he saw another green bubble, beneath their feet this time, very small but growing larger as they sank towards it. Then it was as though they pricked the bubble with their feet, and it burst, and in place of the evening light that they had left behind, the cool light of morning flooded in upon them, and they were standing on solid ground once more.

The instant their feet touched the ground, the dark champion tore himself away from Dearmid's grasp and rushed away. Dearmid would have followed, but the weariness and the wounds of his four day's fighting suddenly rose up and engulfed him, and before he had taken three paces, he sank to the ground and into the deepest and purest and most refreshing sleep that he had known since he was a boy, with the Boyne singing to him all night long as it flowed past his sleeping place.

He was awakened by a light blow on the shoulder, and opened his eyes to see a young man with hair that clung close about his head and neck like a helmet of red gold, an air of command about him such as marked the greatest of the Fian Chiefs in Erin, and in his hand a naked sword. Dearmid sprang to his feet and reached for his own sword, but the young man smiled, and sheathed his blade.

'I am no enemy. I touched you with the flat of my blade to rouse you, for you are sleeping in a dangerous place. Come with me and you shall find somewhere better and safer to have your sleep out.'

'This is a better welcome than I had from another warrior a while back,' said Dearmid, and he and the young man set out together.

If the world above on the island had seemed fair, the world through which Dearmid now walked was fairer still; the birdsong sweeter, the colours of leaf and flower so brilliant that they glimmered as though formed of rainbow light. After a while they came to a splendid dun, whose white walls seemed to shine of themselves as white flowers do at twilight, and where apple trees clustered about the outer walls carrying silver blossom and golden fruit at the same time. They went in, and the young man led Dearmid by side ways that avoided the crowded courts and all the places where people were, to an inner chamber somewhere behind the hall. It seemed that he was the lord of the dun, for when he shouted for servants to heat up water in the biggest cauldron and make all ready for a guest-bath, they came running to do his will; and in no time at all the fire was blown up, and soft linen towels and jars of sweet-smelling unguents were brought in while the water was heating in a great bronze cauldron. When it was hot enough and swung clear of the fire, the young man himself scattered into it balsams and healing herbs, so that when Dearmid stepped into it, instantly his wounds knit up and his weariness fell away from him, and when he had bathed, and stepped out again, he felt as though he had never been weary in all his life and could never be weary in all the rest of it. Meanwhile the lord of the dun had caused Dearmid's tattered and battle-stained clothes to be gathered up and thrown away, and a fine shirt of saffron silk with breeks of the softest chequered stuff and a mantle of crimson silk to be brought in their place. And while Dearmid put them on, they talked together.

'Forgive me if I am asking many questions,' Dearmid said. 'So many strange things have chanced that the very ground seems unsure beneath my feet, and not until I know the who and the where and the why of it, will the ground grow solid again.'

'Ask then, and I will forgive the number of the questions,' said the lord of the dun, smiling.

'What land is this, then? And who was the champion I fought with through four days, at the pool? And, young lord, who are you, who give me the hospitality of your house?'

The other laughed. 'That is three questions to be going on with, and I will answer each in turn. This land is Tir-fa-Thonn, the Land under the Sea, and the champion who you fought with at the pool is its King. As for myself, I am the King's brother — look, and you will remember me, for not long since I took service for a year and a day with Finn Mac Cool, though indeed I served but little of the agreed time.'

As he spoke, he gazed fixedly at Dearmid, and Dearmid returning the gaze, seemed to see someone else forming behind his eyes: a huge fat man with bow legs and a face all over hair, and him dragging a hideous old black horse behind him.

'Why, you — you are the Giolla Dacker!'

'I am indeed,' said the Prince.

'Then here is another question for you. Where are the fifteen of my Fian brothers who you carried off on the back and clinging to the tail of your horse?'

'Safe and well, as you shall see in a while when we gather for this evening's feasting in my hall.'

'And why were you carrying them off at all?'

'Because I had need of them, and of you and the rest of the war-boat's crew that I knew Finn Mac Cool would bring seeking them.'

'What need would that be?' demanded Dearmid.

'Half this kingdom is mine by right, but when our father left the kingship, my brother, who was older and stronger than I, seized my heritage along with his own. But here with me I have seven score heroes who are loyal to me, and here, also, see, I have summoned the very flower of the warriors of Erin. With your help, if you will but give it to me, I shall win back my kingdom and all that was reft from me by my brother. And after, each and every one of you shall claim from me whatever you most desire.'

'For myself, it is a bargain,' Dearmid said. 'My comrades must speak for themselves.'

So Dearmid and the Prince of Tir-fa-Thonn struck hands as men sealing a bargain, and swore faith and loyalty, each to the other.

Meanwhile Finn and the rest of the Fianna who had sailed with him, having waited five days for Dearmid's return, determined to go in search of him. They took all the cables and ropes in the ship, and knotted them together until they had a rope long enough to reach from the bottom to the top of the cliff. Then the two best climbers among them went up the cliff-face, following the way that Dearmid had taken, and carrying the end of the rope with them. And reaching the top at last, they made fast the rope to a jut of rock, so that the rest could climb after them.

When the last warrior was standing safely on the cliff-top grass, they set out through the woods, just as Dearmid had done, but they came out at another point, and so never saw the magic spring that had led Dearmid to his adventure. Instead, they came to a cave among the last of the trees, and since the sun was sinking, they entered it to see if it would make a good shelter for the night.

'It looks both warm and dry,' said Finn, 'but it is never well to sleep in such a place without first finding the far end, lest any danger lurk in the further depths.' So they went in further – and further – and further still, but the cave went on and on, seemingly without any end at all. And they were just about to give up and turn back to camp in the open, when they saw daylight glimmering far ahead of them. So they pushed on towards it, but whereas they had left behind them the honey-glow of sunset, they stepped out from the cave into a cool clear flood of early morning light.

'That is strange,' said Finn. 'We have not been a whole night in the cave, I am as sure of that as I am that the High King of Erin holds his court at Tara.'

But the others were already looking ahead of them, to where at some distance they could see the white walls of a dun on its hill set among apple trees on which the blossom shone silver while the apples were already golden.

On the green grass before the dun, warriors were at practice with swords and shields and spears, and as they drew nearer they saw that among them were Dearmid and the fifteen who had been carried off by the Giolla Dacker. These saw them at the same instant, and set up a great shout, and tossing up their spears came running to meet them.

Great was the gladness and rejoicing on both sides. Then Dearmid brought Finn and his comrades back to the warriors on the practice-ground, and the seven score tall Danann warriors greeted them with courtesy, both they and their women, all in mantles of scarlet silk, who had come out to watch the warrior-play. And at the head of the warriors came the Prince himself, to bid them welcome.

So Finn and the war-boat's crew heard, as the others had done already, the story of why they had been drawn out of Erin to Tir-fa Thonn, and each and every one of them struck hands with the Prince and swore to keep faith with him in the fighting which was to come. And that evening they feasted royally in the Prince's hall, Fian and Danann warriors together, eating from the same dish and drinking from the same wine cup, while the leaping harp-notes hummed under the rafters, as sweetly as the notes of the Dagda's harp itself in the green years when the three Worlds were young.

And next morning, with Finn and the Prince at their head, Fian and Danann warriors together marched out to attack the royal dun.

But Dearmid's old enemy had had word of their march from his scouts, and advanced to meet them. So they came together midway. And the King's war host was many times greater than the war host of the Prince his brother. But the Prince's war host had in it one-and-thirty champions of the Fianna of Erin.

When the two war hosts came in sight of each other, they checked, and drew up their battle line facing each other across a shallow valley, and in the same instant the war horns of Tir-fa-Thonn sang from one side of the valley, and on the other, Finn tossed up his spear glittering in the sunlight, and shouted the Dord Fian, the Fian war cry that was taken up by every voice in the Prince's war host, Danann as well as Fian, and the two battle lines rolled towards each other, while the white dust rose above the warriors and the spear-points rose above the dust.

All that day they fought, without either side gaining an advantage over the other, until towards sunset, the greater numbers of the King's war host began to tell. When Finn saw this happening, he filled his breast and his belly and his throat with air, until he felt his feet grow light beneath him and the world turned red, and with all the power that was in him, he raised the Dord Fian in the way in which it was only sounded when the Fianna were in desperate straits.

As the sound of the Dord Fian fell on his hearing, Dearmid's battle fury rose in him, and he rushed forward against the enemy, not even caring to see that his comrades were at his heels. He hurled himself against the enemy centre, where the silken banners of the King flew in the wind, and went through them and under them and over them as a hawk goes through a flock of sparrows or a whale through a shoal of little fish or like a raging wolf among a flock of sheep. So he broke a red pathway right through the heart of the enemy host, and his comrades raged through after him.

The war host of the King of Tir-fa-Thonn broke apart and crumbled and was put to rout, and the King and his son who fought beside him where both slain. And so at the last red of sunset, the battle ended.

For three days and three nights the Fian warriors feasted with the new King and his people, but at the end of that time Finn wished to return home, for he had left Erin in something of a hurry and Oisīn maybe scarcely old enough to hold command of the whole Fianna.

'It is sorry I am to lose you so soon,' said the new King of Tir-fa-Thonn, 'but if you must go, then you must. Yet first, tell me what rewards you would have of me for your aid in this matter.'

'As I remember,' Finn said, laughing, 'you left my service without claiming your wages – though to be sure you did not serve your full year and a day. Let us set the one against the other, and count all debts paid.'

And the rest agreed to this, all save Conan Maol, who was not so easily satisfied. ' 'Tis all very well for you, who came here in a fine ship, to count all debts paid,' said he glaring at Finn. 'It was not you that felt the sharp bones of that accursed horse under you all the long sea-road from Erin!'

At this, the young King choked with swallowed laughter, and said gravely enough, 'That is true. Choose now what award you would like, and I will pay it whatever it may be.'

'The award that I choose is this,' said Conan, very

pleased with himself, 'that you should set fourteen of your finest warriors upon the brute, and yourself catch hold of the tail, and return to Erin in the same manner and along the same sea-roads by which we came. Then, and only then, I will count the debt paid.'

The Fianna drew breaths of relief, for they had feared that Conan might demand gold or jewels, and so bring shame upon them.

'It is a fair award,' said the King, 'and shall be paid in full. When you reach your own land, wait for us on the hill above Cliach where first you saw the Giolla Dacker and his horse. And we will come to you there.'

So Finn and his men went back through the cave and the woods, and down the cliff by the rope still hanging there, to the waiting war-boat, and set out for home. And when they reached the shores of Erin, they went to the hill where their hunting camp still stood, and waited.

They had not long to wait before they saw the Giolla Dacker, looking more hideous and surly than ever as he trudged towards them, dragging after him his bony mare with the fourteen luckless chieftains on her back, for he had let go of her tail and gone ahead with the halter, the moment they touched the shores of Erin.

The Fianna tried to keep their faces straight for courtesy's sake, but such a gale of laughter caught them that they were still laughing when the mare checked at the place from which she had set out, and the chieftains began stiffly to dismount.

Finn strode gladly forward to meet them, but the Giolla Dacker who was King of Tir-fa-Thonn, looked past him and pointed, 'Finn Mac Cool! Quick and look to your men!' Finn glanced round quickly, but there was nothing amiss with the men. He turned back again, puzzled, to the Giolla Dacker, but the Giolla Dacker was gone, and so was the great black mare, and so were the fourteen nobels of the Land under the Sea. All that was left was the grass springing up again, where the black mare's hooves had crushed it down.

And neither Finn nor Dearmid nor any other of the one-and-thirty ever saw them again.

9

The Horses of the Fianna

This is the story of how the Fianna came by their cavalry horses, for until then, though they had used ponies and little sturdy horses for hunting, they had not used horses in war.

At the time of the story Finn had serving with him in the Leinster Fianna a young champion called Arthur, a lesser son of the King of Britain, who had come overseas to Erin in search of adventure, bringing a company of twenty-eight warriors at his back.

All the tests of the Fianna he had passed with honour; he was brave in battle and skilled on the hunting trail. But if there was a thing he wanted, he took it if he could. And if it belonged to another man, he was not one to trouble much, but took it all the same — especially if there was a dash of danger to make the taking seem more worth while.

He was a good judge of a horse, and more than that he was a good judge of a hound, and he had not been long with the Fianna before he knew that in all Britain and Erin put together there were no two hounds to equal Finn's two hunting favourites, Bran and Skolawn, for speed or strength, beauty or valour or wisdom. And it was not three heartbeats of time after he knew that, that he determined to steal them at the first chance that came his way.

He waited for a while and a while, and then there

were two things happened together: a British trading ship put in to Dublin Bay and Finn Mac Cool decided to hunt on Ben Eader close by.

The hunting camp was made, and the Fianna gathered with their hounds. Now there was no hound pack in the world of men such as the pack that Finn hunted, for between them the Fian chiefs could muster three hundred full-grown hounds, and there were always two hundred puppies coming on to take the place of those that died or grew too old for the chase. The Fianna valued their hunting dogs dearly, and at the end of every day's hunting, when their food was thrown to them, the pack was counted to make sure that no hound had gone astray.

Arthur knew this, but he knew also — having sent one of his warriors with gold to make the thing sure — that the British ship would wait for him and sail the instant that the tide served, after his coming, If he could steal Bran and Skolawn early in the day, and get them down to the ship in time to sail with the noon tide, he could be well on his homeward way with many miles of open sea between himself and Finn before the count was taken in the evening.

So at dawn, when the hunting started, when the deer were stirring in the woods and the hounds stood quivering in leash, he slipped away from the rest, he and his eight-and-twenty followers, and turned hunters themselves. Only beside their spears, each carried three throw-stones joined to each other in a curious way with different lengths of rawhide rope, supple and strong. With these, when the chase had had time to become well scattered, they went hunting Bran and Skolawn.

The two great hound brothers liked always to hunt together, apart from the rest of the pack, and so Arthur knew that if he and his followers could find them at all, there would be a good chance of taking them without the rest of the hunt, hound or man, knowing a thing of what happened, and sure enough, that was how it came about.

Presently, with the trail-music of the pack distant in his ears, Arthur saw a magnificent twelve-point stag in full flight, and knew that with such a splendour of a quarry, and the rest of the pack half across Mide and Leinster by the sound of it, Bran and Skolawn could not be far off; so he signalled with the cry of a late-waking owl three times repeated, to any of his twenty-eight who might be nearest, and himself crouched down behind a low-growing briar tangle. Hardly had he done so than the two great hounds broke from cover, streaking low through the fern and baying as they ran.

There was no moment to wait, no moment, as it looked, to be taking aim, but Arthur was used to capturing game alive with his strange weapon in his own land. He swung the seeming tangle of stones and rawhide thongs once round his head and let go, and the thing flew out straight to its mark, and wrapped itself about Bran, the throw-stones carrying the hide ropes across and across, so that the great hound fell in mid gallop, hopelessly meshed in the thongs about his legs. And in the same instant Skolawn sprawled headlong and lay kicking, brought down by another of the hidden hunters. Their baying changed to snarls of fury as they fought with the hide ropes. Bran was half up again, but men were running in from every side to come at them before they could injure themselves or break free. Arthur himself braved Bran's terrible snapping jaws to leap in with clenched fist and deal him a blow behind the ears that should quieten him for a while. Another of the Britons did the same for Skolawn with the pommel of his dagger. And they stood triumphant with the two hounds lying moveless at their feet.

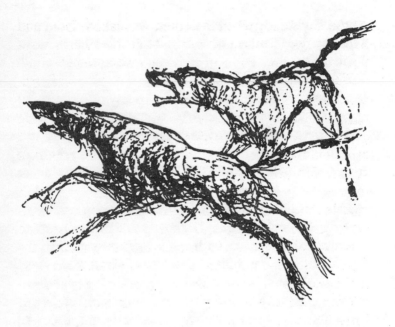

'So far it is good,' Arthur said, 'but I am thinking that the sooner we are away from this place, and from Erin, the better it will be for us, my heroes!'

They untangled the hounds and, because they were too big for any man to carry alone, lashed forepaws together and hindpaws together, and slipped spear shafts between the bound paws of each hound, so that they could lift and carry them, two men to a spear, as men carry home their hunting kill.

Then they set off towards the place where the ship waited.

They went on board, and with Bran and Skolawn already waking back to fury, sailed with the tide, the wind filling their sail and speeding them towards Britain.

At the day's end, when the count was taken, Bran and Skolawn were missing, and though the Fianna went through the pack again and again, and searched all the country round about, not so much as a grey or a brindled hair of them could be found.

Then Finn set his Thumb of Knowledge between his teeth, and the truth came to him, and with the truth came bitter anger. He stood up and looked about him at his hunting companions, and said harsh in his throat, 'Arthur, son of the King of Britain has stolen away my hounds, and they are now on the sea, with a fair wind driving them towards the coast of Britain. Now I call for nine champions to follow and bring them back to me, and Arthur with them — or his head if they cannot be bringing the whole of him!'

Then Goll Mac Morna stood up and said, 'Here am I that will go, for one.'

And Dearmid O'Dyna said, 'A sorry thing it would be to hunt these hills and never again to hear the trail-music of Bran and Skolawn. Here am I that will go, for another.'

And Oisīn slipped his harp bag from his shoulder (for he had brought it out before the count was taken, to sing for the Fianna after supper) and said to Osca his twelve summers old son, who had come hunting with them for the fist time, 'Keep this for me until I come back.'

But Osca drew together his brows that were as black as Finn's and Oisīn's were fair, and said, 'Let you find someone else to keep your harp for you. Many and many a night I have slept between Bran and Skolawn for warmth and company. I come with you to find them and bring them back.'

'You are too young and small,' said Oisīn. 'What could you do?'

Osca grinned, and said, 'I will bite Arthur's ankles and hold him till the rest of you come up.'

And the others laughed, and took his side, and so Oisīn yielded. And Osca took his place among the men for his first foray.

Coil Croda the Hundred-Slayer had joined the little band while they argued, and with him Ferdoman, son of Bodh Derg, and the two brothers Raigne Wide-Eye and Caince the Crimson-Red. And lastly came Cailte, son of Crunnchu; and the nine were complete.

A ship was made ready, and they lime-whitened their shields for battle and put their war-caps on their heads, and went on board. The rowers swung to the oars and the wind filled the square sail and sped them towards Britain. And so they came upon the coast of Argyll. Then they beached the ship safe above the tide-line and went in search of Arthur, the son of the King.

They searched northward and they searched southward, and at last one evening, close to the mountain of Lodan Mac Lir, they saw smoke rising from the hillside and caught on the wind the smell of roasting meat. 'It is only a hunting camp such as we have made often enough ourselves,' said Oisīn.

But Goll Mac Morna said, 'And where would we more likely find Bran and Skolawn than in a hunting camp? Unless it was on the trail? So soon as it is dark, we will be taking a closer look.'

So when the blue dusk rose like water soaking up through the hazel woods, they crept closer, as close as they dared for fear the hunting dogs would get their scent. And crouching among the hillside scrub, they peered between the branch-woven bothies and saw the hunters gathered about the fire, and saw that they were Arthur and his band. And chained to a birch tree in the midst of the camp, all men keeping well clear of them, were Bran and Skolawn.

Then the nine drew back and gathered close together and made their plan. And they spread out into a circle all about the hunting camp, and as each man reached his place, he waited, crouching with his spear across his knee, until in the last place of all, old Goll Mac Morna raised the first shout of the Dord Fian; then they leapt to their feet and rushed in upon the camp from all quarters, yelling as they came.

The men about the fire had scarcely time to snatch up their weapons before they were upon them. The fighting raged about the fire, and into and through the fire so that blazing logs and bright embers were scattered far and wide. And at last the eight-and-twenty were slain to a man, but Arthur they took alive, though with many wounds upon him, for as he sprang aside from a thrust of Dearmid's spear Osca flung himself at his legs and wrapped his arms around them and brought him crashing down. And he hit his head

on a stone in the blood-stained grass, so that he lay
still for a while; and Dearmid and Oisín dragged him
clear of the fighting and bound his hands at his back.

'Did I not say that I would bite his ankles and hold
him for the rest of you to come up?' Osca said.

Then they loosened the chains that held Bran and
Skolawn captive for all their straining and struggling
to join the fight, and the two great hounds leapt about
them barking with the joy of their release.

'Now we will be on our way back to Erin. And all
of Arthur with us, which will please Finn better than
his head alone,' said Dearmid.

But Goll Mac Morna, who had been peering about
him with his one fierce falcon's eye, said, 'Something
else is here also, that we will be taking back with us
to Erin.'

And looking where he looked, they saw two horses
tethered beside the largest of the bothies. So while
some them raked the remains of the fire together and
kicked it into a blaze that there might be light to see
by, Goll and Dearmid went to free their tethers and
bring them out for a closer look.

They were a stallion and a mare, taller and heavier
and more fiery than any horses of the land of Erin, and
they laid back their ears and snorted and plunged at
the strange hands on their bridles, so that it took all
the skill of Goll and Dearmid to get them quietened
and lead them towards the fire at last.

The stallion was a grey with strange tiger-spot
markings, and his bridle and head ornaments were of
reddest gold, and the mare was red, with a bridle of
three-times purified silver and a golden bit.

'These alone would be worth crossing the sea for,'

said Goll Mac Morna, and sighed as a dog sighs, who eats his fill and flings himself down by the fire after a hard day's hunting.

They struck off the heads of the slain and knotted them to their belts by the long hair; three heads at his belt each of the Fian warriors had, except for Goll Mac Morna, who had four. And with Goll and Dearmid riding the red mare and the grey stallion, Bran and Skolawn loping ahead of them, and Arthur captive in their midst, they set out for the place where they had left the war-boat, and they ran it down into the shallows and went on board and set sail for Erin.

It was no easy voyage they had of it. The mare and the stallion were angry and afraid, and more than once came near to capsizing the boat and going to join the white steeds of Manannan the Lord of the Sea — and taking the warriors with them. But at last they came safely to shore on the coast of Erin, and set out for Ben Eader, where Finn was still waiting for them.

'You have been a long time,' said Finn, fondling the ears of Bran and Skolawn while the two great hounds crouched whimpering with joy against his knee.

'It was a long trail we followed,' said Goll, 'but the hunting was good in the end.' And the warriors flung down the heads at the Fian Captain's feet. Osca flung his heads down last of all, and the pride was on him like the dark bloom on the wings of a moth. Then they thrust forward Arthur to stand captive before him, and lastly Goll and Dearmid brought up the two horses, whose like no man had seen in Erin before.

Finn accepted all that they had brought, and he said to the captive Prince, 'Arthur, son of Britt, an ill thing you have done, but I'm not wishing to waste a bold warrior, for all that. If I cut these bonds, will you take back the old bonds that bind all the Fianna? Will you swear fealty again to me, as though it were for the first time and all this had never happened?'

'I will so, and that gladly,' said Arthur. So he swore fealty again to Finn Mac Cool, and followed him faithfully, to the day of both their deaths.

And Finn took the mare and stallion and bred from them. And the mare foaled many times, dropping eight fine foals at every birth. And her foals, and their foals after them, became the cavalry horses of the Fianna, who had had no cavalry before.

10
The Hostel of the
Quicken Trees

Once there was a king of Lochlan whose name was
Colga of the Hard Weapons, for he was a mighty and
a warlike king, and on a day he called his chiefs
together to the broad green before his palace of Berva,
and said to them, 'You know that I am called King of
the Four Tribes of Lochlan and of the Islands of the
Sea. Yet there is an island which does not bow to my
rule, and that is the green island of Erin. Now,
therefore, it is in my mind that when the sailing winds
come we will run the long war-boats down to the sea,
and sail for this Erin, to set the matter right.'

And his chieftains shouted in agreement and beat
upon their shields.

Then the King sent word throughout the land of
Lochlan, calling his war host together; and they ran
the war-boats down into the surf. And with the rowers
straining at the oars and the sailing winds of early
summer filling the great square sails, they set out to
conquer Erin; and so at last they made landfall on the
coast of Ulster.

Cormac Mac Art, High King of Erin, heard of their
landing from his coast watchers, and sent word by his
swifest runners to Finn at the Hill of Almu. Then Finn
sent out runners in his turn, summoning all the Fianna
to meet him at a certain point on the Ulster coast, and

himself led the Leinster companies north to join the hosting.

All together, they marched against the Lochlan men in the strong camp they had raised on the shore. And there between green hills and the pale sea sands the battle joined. And in the thick of the fighting Colga and Osca the son of Oisín came together, shield to shield and sword to sword and eye to glaring eye, and did not break apart until the King of Lochlan lay dead on the trampled shore-grass. The Lochlan men lost heart when they saw their King go down, and though they fought on until evening, they broke at last and ran for their ships, and the Fianna, hard on their heels made red slaughter among them, so that of all those who had sailed from Lochlan to conquer the green island of Erin, only one was left alive. This was Midac, the King's youngest son, who had come with his father on his first wartrail.

He was brought captive before Finn, and because he was so young, Finn did not have him slain, saying, 'Even a wolf cub may be tamed, if he is taken young enough from the lair. He shall be fostered in my own household.' So when the dead were buried and the wounded brought back to Almu of the White Walls, Finn set the fierce and silent boy among his own household, and gave him servants and tutors as though he were his own son, and when he was old enough, even enlisted him in the Fianna.

Midac hunted and feasted with the Fian warriors, and fought in their ranks when it was time for fighting. But he remained silent and aloof, and made no friends among them.

One day Conan Maol said to Finn, 'Captain, there is such a thing as being too trusting.'

'Is there so?' said Finn.

'Have you never thought that Midac of Lochlan has little cause to love you?'

'I have treated him no better and no worse than my own sons, since the day that he was taken captive.'

'Yet it was by you that his father and all his kin were slain, and the men of Lochlan know how to hate well and long. Midac has no friends among the Fianna, he talks with no one, but he is for ever watching and listening. He is at great pains to find out all that has to do with the defence of Erin. And in Lochlan there are still mighty chieftains with many ships and war bands to fill them. Therefore I say that there is such a thing as being too trusting.'

Finn did not take the matter very deeply, knowing, as all the Fianna knew, that Conan Maol never said a good word when he could say an ill one. But he thought for a while, and it seemed to him that all the same, there was sense in what his fat warrior said.

'What would you advise, then?' he said at last.

'Get him clear of Almu,' said Conan. 'Since it is only fitting that he should still be treated as a prince, give him land of his own, and cattle, and a house and household; but let it be in some other part of Erin, where he cannot be listening to all our councils.'

Finn went away and thought again. And then he sent for him, and said, 'Midac, you have been brought up from boyhood in my household, and trained as I trained my own sons, but now you are a man, and the time for training is past, and you should be having a land-holding and household of your own. Choose the two holdings that best please you in all Erin, and they shall be yours and your sons' after you with cattle and slaves.'

Midac listened to the Fian Captain in cold silence, and answered in a voice as cold as his silence. 'The Lord of the Fianna is generous. If I may have my choice of all the holdings in Erin, I will have the Holding of Kenri on the Shannon, and the Holding of the Islands north of it across the river.'

His answer came so quickly that Finn knew that he had had the matter thought out already, and he guessed the reason for Midac's choice — for between those two holdings the Shannon widened into a great firth set with islands and many sheltered creeks, and a whole Lochlan fleet could lie there in safety.

But he could not break his word. So Midac had the holdings of his choice, and the cattle and the slaves, and built his house and lived there. He lived there fourteen years, and in all that time neither the High King nor Finn nor any other of the Fianna saw him or had word of him.

And then one day Finn and the Fianna went to hunt in the woods towards Kenri. But when all was made ready for the hunting, Finn, as he sometimes did, decided to watch the sport from the top of the hill of Knockfierna, where the hunting camp was being made ready, and some of his companions remained with him, while the rest took the hounds and scattered in search of wolf or wild boar.

Presently the men on the hill top saw coming up towards them a tall and splendid warrior clad in a shirt of Lochlan ring-mail, his shield on his shoulder, his two war spears in his right hand. He came to a stand before Finn, and saluted him in all courtesy. 'Greeting to you, Finn Mac Cool, Lord of the Fianna.'

And Finn returned the greeting. 'And to you, friend-and-stranger, if you will tell us what name to call you by.'

But Conan cut in. 'Neither friend nor stranger. Men change in fourteen years, Captain, but do you not know Midac of Lochlan, whom you brought up at your own hearth?'

'Surely I know him now,' Finn said, 'and by your looks you have grown to be the most noble champion in the Five Provinces. But in all these fourteen years we have had no word of you.'

'And never in all that time,' put in Conan with rising indignation, 'has he invited you or any of his old comrades to eat beneath his roof!'

Midac answered pleasantly enough, 'If Finn and the Fianna have not feasted with me, surely that is none of my fault; there was never a time when they would not have been welcome.' He smiled and held out his free hand. 'But now you are come, and there is a feast waiting for you. I have had it set out in my guest hostel, the Hostel of the Quicken Trees, which is nearer than my dun, which I have built on one of the islands for greater strength in time of trouble.'

Finn agreed gladly to go and feast with him, and after pointing out their way, Midac left them, saying that he must go on ahead to make sure all things were in order.

When he was gone, the companions on the hill top held council together, and it was decided that Oisín, with Dearmid O'Dyna, and Fotla and Keelta Mac Ronan, and a young son of Finn's called Ficna with

his foster-brother Innsa, should remain to tell the rest
of the hunting party when they returned, and bring
them on down, while Goll Mac Morna and Conan and
some others went down with Finn to the Hostel. And
it was decided also that Finn should send back word
of how they fared.

Finn and his companions set out, following the way
that Midac had pointed out to them, and after walking
for a good while, they came to a fine and splendid
hostel standing in the midst of a level green and
surrounded by quicken trees lit with clusters of
flaming berries. A river flowed close by, and a path
led down the steep and rocky slope to it, at a place
where there was a ford.

And the strange thing was that for all the size and
splendour of the place, not a living soul was to be seen.
Not a thing moved save the river water and a little
wind that swayed the scarlet clusters of the quicken
trees. Then Finn smelled danger, and he would have
turned back, only that he had given his promise.

The great door stood wide open, and he went in, the
others behind him.

They had never seen a hall so splendid, not even in
the High King's palace at Tara. A great fire burned on
the hearth, bright and smokeless and sweet-scented;
the walls were hung with fine embroidered webs of
blue and violet and crimson, and all round the hall
were couches spread with brilliant rugs and deep rich
furs. But here also there was no living soul. Nothing
moved but the flames of the fire.

Still wondering the meaning of this, they seated
themselves on the couches, and hardly had they done
so when one of the inner doors opened, and Midac

stood there. He looked them over, speaking no word. A long look to each and every one. Then he turned on his heel and went out shutting the door again behind him.

Finn and his companions waited a while longer with uneasiness growing upon them. At last Finn said, 'I am thinking it a strange thing, that we should have been bidden to a feast, and kept so long without food or drink.'

'It is in my mind that there is a thing stranger still,' said old Goll Mac Morna, suddenly. 'The hearth fire, which was clear and smokeless and scented as a may tree in flower when we entered this place, is now filling the hall with foul black smoke!' he began to cough.

And that was not the only change, for in the same instant the beautiful hangings fell away in a shower of withered leaves from the walls that were only rotten planks; the couches with their soft coverings were gone, so that the warriors were now sitting on bare black earth that was cold as the first snows of winter. And the many doors had disappeared, leaving only the one that they had come in by, and that one shrunk to half its size and closely fastened.

Then Finn said, 'I never tarry in a house that has only one way out. Let one of you break down the door and we will be out of this foul smokey den.'

'That's a thing easily done,' said Conan, and made to scramble to his feet, then fell back with a howl. 'Help me! Oh friends, help! I'm fixed to this cold clay floor as though I were rooted here like the quicken trees!'

And when they would have gone to his aid, all the

rest found themselves fast to the ground in the same manner. For three heart-beats of time, the shock of it held them frozen silent. Then Goll said harshly, 'Midac has laid a trap and we have walked into it. Quick, Finn, put your Thumb of Knowledge between your teeth, that we may know what we face, and how to escape from this ugly plight.'

So Finn put his thumb between his teeth and waited for the knowledge, and then he gave a deep and bitter groan. 'Fourteen years has Midac, son of the King of Lochlan, plotted against us, and now his plotting has come to its harvest time, and I can see no way to escape for us. For in the Dun of the Island, he has even now a war host gathered to destroy the Fianna. It is led by Sinsar of the Battles, King of the World, and his son Borba the Haughty, and with them are the three Kings of the Island of the Torrent, strong and fierce as three dragons, and mighty in magic-making. It is they who by their black spells have made us fast here, and we can never be set free until the blood of all three of them is sprinkled on this earthen floor. And soon, Sinsar's warriors will be here to make an end of us — and we are as helpless as trussed fowls to defend ourselves.'

Then Conan Maol (who, let you remember, had been held captive in this way before, and had a ram's fleece down his back to prove it), began to rage and lament, until Finn silenced him. 'It is not fitting for heroes to wail like women or howl like dogs at full moon, in the shadow of death. Rather let us raise the war chant, the Dord Fian, that it may strengthen and put heart into us before we die.'

So all together, they raised the Dord Fian that was

half war-song, half battle cry, chanting slowly and proudly and terribly, as men before a battle that they know can have only one end.

Oisīn and the party waiting on the hill of Knockfierna grew anxious when evening came and still there was no sign of the messenger Finn had promised to send back. And Ficna got to his feet and said that he would go down to the Hostel of the Quicken Trees, and see for himself how it went with his father, and Innsa his foster-brother rose to go with him.

It was nightfall when they reached the Hostel but there were no lights anywhere. And as they drew near, from the dark and seemingly forsaken hall ahead of them, they heard the loud slow strain of the Dord Fian coming from within.

'At least they are here in this place, and safe,' said Innsa.

But Ficna shook his head. 'It is only in time of sorest danger that Finn my father raises the Dord Fian in manner so slow and stately-grim.'

Now as the war-song fell silent, Finn, within their prison, heard the hushed, quiet voices outside, and called out, 'Is that Ficna?'

'Yes, my father.'

'Come no nearer, my son, for this place teams with evil magic.' And quickly and urgently Finn told all that had happened, and how only the blood of the three Kings could save him and his companions. At that, Innsa cried out, and hearing him, Finn demanded who else was there.

'It is Innsa, your foster-son.'

'Then fly, both of you, while there is still time, for

it will not be long before our enemies come carrying their swords this way!'

But both young men refused to seek their own safety. 'For while we are here,' said Ficna, 'at least there are two warriors free to stand between you and our foes.'

Then Finn sighed a great sigh, and said, 'So be it then. Every man's fate is written on his forehead . . . Now listen; to reach this place the foreigners must cross the river that runs below here. The ford is narrow, and the banks on this side steep and rocky, and one man might hold it against many — for a while. Go now, and hold that ford, and it may yet be that help will come in time.'

So the two young warriors went down to the ford. And when they had taken stock of the place, Ficna said, 'It is even as my father said; one man might hold this place against many. So now, let you guard the ford alone for a while, and I will go to the island, and if it is not already too late, find if there be any way in which the war host might be attacked before they set out.'

And he went across the ford and on into the night, while Innsa remained behind, leaning on his sword and waiting.

In the Dun of the Island there was feasting and great merrymaking at the news that Midac brought, and one of the chieftains of the King of the World whispered to another chieftain, his brother, 'I am away now while they are all drinking, to the Hostel of the Quicken Trees. But soon I shall be back, bearing the head of Finn Mac Cool. So I shall gain much renown, and win the high favour of the King.'

And he gathered his own war band, and set out. When they came to the ford, it was black night, but peering across the water, the chieftain thought he saw the shape of a warrior on the far side, and called out to know who it might be.

'I am Innsa, of the house of Finn Mac Cool,' came back the answer.

And the chieftain laughed and said, 'Well met! For we are come on a visit to Finn Mac Cool now, to take his head back to our King. And it's yourself will be just the man to lead us to him.'

'That would be a strange way of carrying out my orders, which are to hold this ford against all comers.'

Then the warriors plunged into the ford, and came wading across to the attack, but only two at a time could come at the single defender, and he struck them down, right and left, until the ford was clogged with bodies. At last the few who were left broke off the fight, and fell back to the opposite bank, where their chieftain had been standing all this while, looking on. The chieftain was filled with red rage that so many of his men had fallen without gaining the ford, and snatching up his weapons he rushed into the water himself, against the solitary warrior who held the other bank. He was fresh, but Innsa was weary and sore wounded, and at last he missed his stroke and the enemy chieftain's sword found his breast, and he stumbled forward with a choking cry into the swift running water. Then the chieftain seized him by the long hair, and struck off his head and brought it away.

The few warriors left to him were not, he thought, enough to press on to the Hostel of the Quicken Trees, so he had better be turning back, to take Innsa's head to the King of the World.

But on his way, he met Ficna returning to the ford, and because he came from the Dun of the Island, thought that he must be one of their own men. So he told him triumphantly, 'We are back from the ford below the Hostel of the Quicken Trees. There we met a young champion who slew so many of my warriors that I have had to return for more — yet I do not come empty-handed, for, see, I bring his head with me. I had hoped to bring Finn Mac Cool's, but this is better than no head at all.'

And he tossed the severed head to Ficna as though it had been a ball.

Ficna caught and looked at it, and said, 'Alas, dear old lad. At dusk your eyes were bright with valour.' Then he laid the head aside that it might not hamper him, and turned wrathfully upon the enemy chieftain. 'Do you know who I am, to whom you have tossed this champion's head?'

'I know that you come from the Dun of the Island.' A hideous doubt crept upon the chieftain. 'Are you not, then, a warrior of the King of the World?'

'Not I,' said Ficna, 'nor shall you be, in a few breaths' time,' and he sprang with his raised spear upon the chieftain, swift and savage as a mountain cat. So the chieftain fell by the avenging hand of Ficna, whose foster brother he had slain. And Ficna struck off his head, and taking it by the hair in his left hand, but Innsa's cradled in the crook of this right arm, he went his way.

When he came to the ford, he made a shallow grave and buried Innsa there, his head laid once more to his

shoulders, and turned the green sod back over all. But
the enemy chieftain's head he carried with him, on up
to the Hostel of the Quicken Trees.

Finn, who heard his step and knew it, called out to
him with wild anxiety, 'Ficna, who fought the battle
that we heard raging at the ford? How has it ended?'

'Innsa fought that battle, and the ford is clotted with
the bodies of the men he slew.'

'And how is it with Innsa?'

'Dead where he fought,' said Ficna.

'And you stood by to see it happen?'

'Ochone! Ochone! Would that I had been there to
fight at his shoulder,' cried Ficna, sharp in his throat,
'but I was elsewhere. At least he does not lie
unavenged, for I met the man who struck the blow
soon after, and it is his head that I carry in my hand.'

Then Finn bowed his head on his knee and wept.
'I have good sons, both of blood and fosterage,' he said
at last. 'Now go back to guard the ford, and victory
be on your blade. Maybe help will still come in time.'

So Ficna went down again to the ford.

Meanwhile in the Dun of the Island, another chieftain
called Kirom, the brother of the first, wondered why
his brother did not return, and gathered his own band,
and set out to seek him.

When they came to the ford, they saw the dead men
choking it, and the figure of one solitary champion on
the further side. And Kirom called across to know who
he was, and who had made the slaughter there.

And the answer came back, 'I am Ficna, son of Finn
Mac Cool, and as to the slaughter here, I would not
be asking, if I were you, for the question raises the

wrath in me, and that will be a bad thing for you, if you come at this side of the ford.'

Then Kirom and his warriors rushed the ford, and flung themselves upon Ficna. But Ficna did with them as Innsa had done, until only one man was left, who escaped and ran back to the Dun of the Island with word of what had passed. And Ficna sat down on the bank, covered with blood and very weary.

When the survivor reached the Dun and told his story, Midac of Lochlan was coldly angry, saying that the two chiefs had brought their deaths on themselves and their men, for they had neither the strength nor the courage to meet the champions of the Fianna, and should have known it. 'But now,' said he, 'I will take a band of my own bravest men, the men of Lochlan, and cross the ford no matter who guards it, and slay Finn Mac Cool and his comrades with my own hands.' So he gathered his war band, and set out, and came to the ford, and Ficna on guard on the other side.

First he tried smooth talk. 'Ficna, my heart is warm to be seeing you again, for when I was of Finn's household you never used me ill, nor struck at man or dog that were mine.'

'Nor did any other of the household, or of the Fianna.' Ficna retorted. 'Kindness you had of us all, but especially of Finn my father; and it is a strange way you have of repaying him!'

So then Midac tried threats, and ordered the young champion aside from the ford.

But Ficna only laughed. 'You are many to my one. Surely it can make little difference to you, that I stand in your path! Come, then, and I will give you the warmest welcome in my power!'

Then all happened just as it had happened twice already at the ford. And just as Kirom had done, Midac in red rage at seeing his men struck down, hitched up his shield and charged forward to meet the one defender in single combat, since none of his men could stand against him.

On the hill top where he waited, Oisīn was growing more and more anxious as the night wore on to dawn, and Ficna and Innsa did not return, and he said so to Dearmid O'Dyna.

'This was in my mind also, and I think I will be taking a walk down to the Hostel of the Quicken Trees, and see that all is well down there,' said Dearmid.

'And I also,' said Fotla. And so they went together, by the way the others had taken, but before they reached the quicken trees, they heard the clash of weapons somewhere ahead of them.

'That is Ficna,' Dearmid said, 'for I know his war shout, and he is sore beset.'

They began to run, side by side, and coming on the last lift of the ground, saw the ford below them in the grey dawn light, clogged with dead men, and Ficna and Midac locked in single combat, thigh deep in water. And at the same instant they saw that Ficna was hard pressed and sore wounded, sheltering behind his shield and beginning to give back.

Still running, with his heart bursting in his breast Fotla cried out, 'Dearmid your spear! We cannot reach him in time. Throw, man, your aim is surer than mine —'

'In this light — I may hit the wrong man.'

'You never yet missed your throw. It is the only chance!'

And so, without slackening his headlong speed, Dearmid set his finger on the silken loop of his spear, and threw. The spear flew straight to its mark. It took Midac below the breast bone and stood out a head span beyond his back. But he yelled and thrust forward like a boar pierced by the hunter's spear, and the moment before Dearmid and Fotla reached them, he made a last mighty sword stroke, and Ficna went down before it, while Midac, his last strength gone, crashed forward across the young warrior's body.

Dearmid stood looking down at Ficna's body lying in the shallows of the ford. Then he put out his foot and rolled Midac aside. The last of life still lingered in the Lochlan prince, and he groaned.

'If I had found you dead, I would have passed you by,' Dearmid said, 'but since I find you living, your head shall make some little payment to Finn Mac Cool for his son's death.'

And with one quick stroke of his sword, he smote off Midac's head.

Then, leaving Fotla to guard the ford, he turned and went up through the rocks towards the Hostel of the Quicken Trees, swinging Midac's head by the hair as he went. When he reached the Hostel he shouted and hammered at the door, for the rage was still red in him. And Finn called to him knowing his voice, 'Keep out of this place, for it crawls with foul magic. But tell us who fought the last battle at the ford. We heard the shouting and the weapon-clash, and we know nothing more.'

'Ficna your son fought that battle, single-handed against a whole war band.'

'And how is it with Ficna now?'

'He is dead,' said Dearmid, 'Slaughtered when he was weary and sore wounded, by Midac of Lochlan. I was too late to prevent it, but I have taken vengeance for him, and it is Midac's head that I have in my hand.'

For a long time Finn was silent. And when at last he spoke, his voice was heavy with grief. 'Victory and strength to you, Dearmid. Often have you been the saving of the Fianna when we were in sore straits. But never have I, the Fian Captain, or those with me been in such deadly peril as this. For here we sit, held captive by enchantment, and nothing can free us save the blood of the three Kings of the Island of the Torrent, if it be sprinkled while still warm, on the ground all about us. Meanwhile we are helpless even to defend ourselves. Therefore our only hope is that you should guard the ford until sunrise, when surely the rest of the Fianna will have returned from their hunting and come to your aid.'

'Fotla is at the ford now,' Dearmid said, 'and he and I together will hold it against all comers, till three sunrises hence, if need be.' And he was turning away to go back to the ford when Conan Maol let out a groan that checked him in his tracks.

'Miserable was the hour in which I came to this place, and cold as seashore ice is the earthen floor that holds me captive; but worst of all is to be so long without food or drink, while all the while there will be food and wine for an army no further off than the Dun of the Island. Oh Dearmid, if ever we took the oath of brotherhood that binds all the Fianna, get me some of that food, for I can bear the hunger pains in my belly no more.'

Dearmid struck his spear butt on the ground. 'An

enemy war host seeks your death, and the deaths of Finn and all those with you in there, and only Fotla and myself to hold the ford against them. Is that not enough work for two men? Must I then leave Fotla to hold the ford alone while I go running my neck into needless hazard to steal food for a glutton?'

'If I were a maiden with blue eyes and golden hair, you would make a different answer. But you have always hated me, and many an ill turn you have done me; and now you are well pleased that I should die of hunger in this place!'

'Och then,' said Dearmid, 'let you stop this snapping and snarling, and I will try to get you the food. Anything is better than to be made deaf by the wagging of that evil tongue of yours.'

He went back to Fotla and told him how the thing stood, and that he must guard the ford alone for a while, and went on towards the Dun of the Island.

It was low water, and the sand and shingle made a causeway so that he was able to reach the island almost dry shod. As he drew near, he heard loud drunken voices and all the uproar of a feast that has reached its height, and creeping to the door, he looked in, and saw the great hall crowded with warriors, and the King of the World with his son beside him in the High Place, and many servants going to and fro with great chargers of food and drinking horns brimming with wine.

Dearmid slipped through the outer doors, and took his stand in the shadows of the foreporch, close beside the inner door, and waited his chance, sword in hand. Soon, one of the servants passed close to him, and swift as a salmon's leap. Dearmid struck off his head and caught the wine horn from his hand as he fell, so that not a drop was spilled. Then sheathing his sword, he walked into the hall and straight up to the High Table, picked up one of the serving dishes, and went out through the great door into the night bearing the food and drink with him; and in all the noise and drinking, no one noticed him or wondered at what he did.

When he reached the ford once more, he found Fotla asleep on the bank, and was half minded to rouse him with a kick, but thinking to himself that the young warrior was worn out with toil and watching, he left him there and went on up to the Hostel with the food for Conan Maol.

The next question was how to get the food to the fat warrior, but he managed it at last by tossing it in to him piece by piece, through a chink in the rotten wall, and when Conan had wolfed down the last mouthful, never so much as offering a bite to his leader and comrades, Dearmid got on the roof and broke a hole in the tattered thatch directly over where he sat captive on the floor, and poured the wine down into his great open mouth till it was gone to the last drop.

Then Dearmid went back to the ford, and found all quiet, and Fotla still asleep, and sat down beside him.

When tidings of the death of Midac and his war band reached the Dun of the Island, the three Kings of the Island of the Torrent were filled with black fury that he had gone against Finn without telling them. 'It is our spells that hold him and his companions captive in the Hostel of the Quicken Trees,' they said, 'and ours by right is the killing. And now before some other chieftain thinks to try his spear, we will go and do our own killing!'

So they gathered a strong war band and set out. They came to the ford, and saw in the dim first light of day, the shape of a warrior standing guard on the further side. With one voice they called across to him to know who he was.

Back came the answer. 'I am Dearmid O'Dyna, and one of the champions of Finn Mac Cool, and I wait here to hold the ford against all comers.'

At first they tried speaking him fair, bidding him to leave the ford and no harm should come to him, but Dearmid would have none of that. 'Finn and his companions are under my shield till sunrise. And I do not stir from this place while I live.'

Then the foremost of the enemy rushed upon Dearmid, but he stood against them as a rock stands against a boiling sea, and struck them down as they came, more and more of them thrusting forward into the gaps left by their fallen comrades; and in the midst of the battle, Fotla started up from his sleep and glaring wildly about him, caught up his sword. He shouted to Dearmid, furious that the other had not wakened him, but Dearmid bade him keep his anger for their foes, and Fotla ran upon them so that they went down before him like ripe barley before a hail storm.

Then the three Kings, seeing their men falling left and right, set up a great yelling, and themselves charged into the ford. Dearmid met them, and they fought together until their shields were hacked and their war gear broken and their hot blood ran down. And one by one Dearmid slew the three Kings, while

Fotla with his sword-play held the enemy off from him.

When all was over, the two champions stood breathing in great gasps, and bleeding from a score of wounds. And then Dearmid remembered what Finn had told him as to the breaking of the spell, and he cut off the heads of the three Kings and knotted them together by their hair, and then, Fotla behind him, went back to the Hostel of the Quicken Trees.

As they drew nearer, Finn shouted to them from within, desperate to know the outcome of the latest fighting. And Dearmid shouted back, 'Well and truly have we held the ford, Fotla and I. We have slain the three Kings of the Island of the Torrent, and I hold their three heads warmly bleeding in the hollow of my shield. How shall I bring them to you?'

'Victory and strength to you! Never had the Fianna of Erin two more valiant champions. Let you sprinkle some of the blood on the door.'

Dearmid did as he was bid, and as the crimson drops spattered upon the timbers, the door crashed back, and he saw Finn and his companions still captive upon the floor. Dearmid made all haste to sprinkle the ground about them, and as the bright drops fell hissing upon the earth, each of the captives groaned and struggled to his feet, weary and stiff, but free. They flung their arms about the two champions in thankfulness. But the danger was not yet past, for though they were indeed loosed from the magic bonds, Finn and his companions had scarcely more strength than hour-old calves.

'Not until the sun rises clear of the hills, and the last of this foul magic falls away, shall we have strength to draw sword,' Finn groaned. 'Therefore the ford is still yours to guard, my brothers. Hold until sunrise, and then we shall surely come to relieve you.'

So Dearmid and Fotla went back to the ford yet one time more.

After the last fighting, the few of the enemy to escape carried word of what had happened back to the Dun of the Island. Then Borba the Haughty rose up and said, 'It must be that the Island of the Torrent breeds feeble warriors. Now I will take my own men and avenge the death of so many of the war host, and I will bring back the head of Finn Mac Cool to lay at my father's feet.' (For those who brought back word of the battle did not know that Finn and his companions were freed, though still lacking all their strength.)

So Borba gathered the boldest and best of his warriors and set out, and came to the ford.

Dearmid and Fotla saw them coming, a black, spear-barbed mass of warriors behind their shields, and felt the ground shake as they drew near, and knew that sorely out-numbered as they had been before, never until now had such a war host as this come down to the ford. And Dearmid spake quickly to young Fotla beside him: 'Now is the time for cunning and wariness more than for valour. When they try to rush us, do not be troubling too much to kill, but to keep yourself in one piece behind your shield, for the longer we can hold them in weapon-play, the more chance we have of victory, with the sky already bright in the East, and Finn himself coming to our aid with the sunrise!'

So the two champions fought a waiting fight there at the ford, crouched behind their battered shields, against the dark wave of warriors that crashed upon them. Sometimes they slew, but more often they parried, and never did they yield back a toe's length of ground.

The sky grew light, and lighter yet, and at last the sun rose clear of the hills, and like an old cloak, the spell-cast weakness fell from the men who waited among the quicken trees. 'Now!' cried Finn, and they drew their weapons and sprang up like the sun, and ran for the ford, while the swiftest among them set off like the March wind to take the call for help to Oisín at Knockfierna.

Dearmid and Fotla, still fighting their waiting battle at the ford, heard the war shout behind them, and a rush of feet, and knew that Finn and his companions had come, and their hearts leapt within them, as they drove home their own attack. But the enemy sprang to meet them, and the fighting thickened to a red tempest of blows. And in the midst of it, grim Goll Mac Morna and the proud young prince came together, and as they fought, Goll's battle fury rose until nothing and no man could stand against him, and with one last mighty blow he hacked the head from Borba's shoulders and sent it bounding across the water like a boy skimming stones on a pond.

When they saw their leader drop Borba's warriors lost heart and began to yield, and one of their number sprang back and sped his way to the Dun of the Island, shouting to Sinsar of the Battles how his son was slain and his war host hard pressed by Finn himself, and beginning to give ground.

And the King of the World, leaving his grief for a later time rose and summoned his whole war host to the very last fighting man, and marched for the ford with vengeance in his heart.

All the Fianna had returned from their hunting and were with Oisín when Finn's messenger reached the camp on Knockfierna, and panted out his whole terrible story. And instantly every man caught up his weapons and marched for the Hostel of the Quicken Trees. They came in sight of the ford just as the King of the World came down towards it from the far side. And when they saw each other, both war hosts checked to put themselves into battle array. The Fianna divided off into their five bands, with Finn himself at the head of Clan Bascna leading the Leinster

men, and Goll leading Clan Morna and the Connacht
companies. They advanced, each man with his long
spear in his hand and his sword loose in its sheath. And
as they advanced, so the war host of the King of the
World advanced, darkening all the hill side with their
numbers.

When they came within range, the throw-spears
began to fly between them, and great gaps were torn
in the ranks on either side, before ever the battle
joined; then they drew their swords and rushed upon
each other, meeting in the midst of the ford, and the
water boiling all about them with the thresh of battle.
Finn seemed in all places at once, his great voice clear
as a war horn above the tumult, and wherever he was,
men gathered fresh strength and courage, and thrust
forward, scattering their enemies before them.

But the King of the World was encouraging his own
men in the same way, and wherever his silken standard
flew, they in their turn gathered heart and flung
themselves afresh upon the Fianna.

And now young Osca, son of Oisín, pausing an
instant to rest on his sword, saw the King's standard
and the surge forward that followed it, and his heart
burst into flame within him, and with a great shout,
he rushed upon the warriors who surrounded the King.

When Sinsar of the Battles saw him coming, he
ordered his bodyguard to stand back, and a grim joy
lifted his heart, for there would be a fine vengeance
in slaying this grandson of Finn's with his own hands.
And at first sight, Osca seemed so slight and young
that he thought the vengeance would be easy. So he
waited till Osca was almost upon him, and then sprang
forward to make an end swiftly. Osca was taken by

surprise and reeled back, then gathered himself and stood his ground, giving blow for blow until the clash of their blades rang all up and down the river glen, and the sparks flew as though from a forge fire, and even the battle-locked warriors all about them checked to watch. And for a while it seemed that Osca could make no headway against the King. Then the young champion called in his heart on the valour of his forefathers, and strung himself for one mighty effort, and swung his sword and brought it sweeping sideways in a blow that sheared through mail and buckler, so that the King's head leapt from his shoulders and went downstream after his son's!

At the sight, the Fianna set up a triumphant shout, and again surged forward. And before this new assault, the foreign war host gave back — and back — and broke and streamed away with the Fian warriors baying on their heels and slaughtering as they went. Only a handful of the enemy escaped to the coast, and their ships, to carry back to their own country word of the death of their King and his whole war host.

11
Dearmid and Grania

Now at the time of this story, Finn was beginning to grow old, and his second wife Manissa, daughter of Garad of the Black Knee, was some while dead. And he began to wish to take a third wife, for when he had no woman beside him, he remembered Saba the mother of Oisīn too well. Oisīn understood this and said to him one day, 'If you wish for another wife, my father, why be without one? There is not a maiden worth the having in all green Erin who will not think herself happy if you crook your little finger at her.'

Then Dering Mac Doba, he who had the Inner Sight, said, 'I could name you a maiden in all ways worthy to be your wife.'

'And who is she.'

'She is Grania, daughter of Cormac the High King, and the most beautiful of all the maidens of Erin.'

'Then let you and Oisīn go to Tara, and ask the High King for the maiden, to sit by my hearth,' said Finn, not much caring which way the thing went.

So Oisīn and Dering set out for Tara, and were made welcome by Cormac the High King. But when they told him their errand, he said, 'There is scarcely a prince or chieftain in all Erin who has not come seeking my daughter in marriage, and she has refused them all and made it seem that it was I who refused them. She has made me more than enough of enemies thereby, and I am weary of it. Ask her yourselves, and so *this* time at least, I shall not get the blame if she refuses.'

Then he took them to the women's apartments on the sunny side of the palace, and there they found the Princess, tall and dusky-fair as a white-throated fox-glove, sitting on a couch with all her maidens about her, stringing beads of yellow amber into a girdle. And when they had told her their errand from Finn Mac Cool, she went on stringing the amber beads, and said, clearly without much thought to the matter, 'If he seems a worthy son-in-law to you, my father, then I suppose he will do well enough for a husband for me.'

So Oisín and Dering returned to Almu of the White Walls, with word for Finn that the Princess Grania had accepted him, and he was to go to Tara in two weeks' time, to bring away his bride.

The two weeks passed, and with the chiefs and champions of the Fianna for his bodyguard (and never was any man having a prouder or more splendid bodyguard) Finn rode to Tara to claim his bride.

Cormac the King greeted them with good honour, and that night there was feasting in the high hall of Tara, and at the feasting, the High King sat in his chair of state, with the Queen at his left hand and Finn at his right, and Grania sat beside the Queen her mother. And while it could be seen that Finn turned often in his seat for a glimpse of Grania, after their first meeting she scarcely looked at him at all. Dara of the Poems, one of Finn's Druids, sat at her left and presently she began to talk to him.

'This is fine company gathered in my father's hall, but save for Oisín I know none of them, being so newly judged old enough to come out from the women's court at times like these. Tell me, then, who is the grim old warrior with one eye?'

'That is Goll Mac Morna the Terrible in Battle,' said Dara.

'And the young champion on his right?'

'That is Osca the son of Oisĩn.'

'Who then, is the chief built like a greyhound?'

'That is Keelta Mac Ronan, the swift-footed.'

Grania was silent a moment, then she asked: 'And the champion with the dark hair and the fair skin and the mole on his brow, who looks as though he could be both gentle and terrible. Who is that one?'

'That is Dearmid O'Dyna, Dearmid of the Love Spot. Do not look too hard, for it is said that all women who look his way are apt to fall in love with him.'

But Grania went on looking, and presently she called one of her handmaidens to her, and said, 'Go and fetch me the chased drinking horn from my chamber,' and then whispered something in her ear, which was heard by no other soul.

And when the girl brought it, no one except Grania saw the few drops of blood-red liquid already in the bottom of the horn. She filled it to the brim from the great wine vat on the table then gave it back to her maiden, saying, 'Take this to Finn Mac Cool from me, and tell him that I would have him drink from my own horn.'

Finn took the cup and drank, bending his head to her, then passed the wine-horn to the High King, who drank likewise and passed it to his Queen. And after that, Grania bade her maiden to take it to the Prince her brother, Cairbri of the Liffey, and so on until all who she wished had drunk from the horn. And in a little while a soft deep sleep fell upon them all.

Then Grania rose from her seat, and walked straight down the hall and sat herself beside Dearmid, and looking into his eyes said, 'Dearmid O'Dyna, if I were to give you my love, would you give me yours to fill the place it left empty in my heart?'

Dearmid straightened at the table and his eyes flew wide. For one moment before he was on guard against her his heart leapt with joy, like a bird waking in his breast. Then he remembered his duty to his chief. 'The maiden who is Finn Mac Cool's cannot be Dearmid O'Dyna's.'

Grania lowered the white lids over her eyes and looked on the floor. But she never thought of giving up what she had so suddenly found. 'I know that was your duty, and not your heart that spoke, or I should not be daring to say more. But you see how it is with me. Finn is a great hero and any maiden would be honoured to be sought by him, but he is as old as my father, and I do not love him. You, who are young, as I am, must surely pity me, and listen when I beg you to save me from becoming his wife.'

Then Dearmid was sore troubled, for indeed his love had gone out from him to the Princess Grania, and to hear her plead for his help and have to refuse it, was like a knife turning in a wound; but he still held firm to his loyalty, and answered her coldly, 'You made the choice of your own free will. And if you cannot see that a man is not less worth loving because he has soldiered through more years than another man, what is that to me?' And then he burst out, 'And even if I were to be as false to him as you are, and did as you would have me do, there is not a fastness in all Erin that would shelter us from the wrath of Finn!'

'So, so,' said Grania. 'I have tried one way, now I will try another. I lay you under geise, under the bonds that no hero may break and save his honour and his soul, that you take me with you out of Tara before Finn and his companions waken from their sleep.' She rose to her feet. 'At moonrise I will be waiting for you at the wicket gate that leads out from the women's court. If you do not come, I will fly from Tara alone, but the geise I leave on your head.'

And turning she left the hall.

Dearmid turned to the few friends closest to him, who had not been given the drugged wine, and who had sat in silence, seeing and hearing all that went on. 'Oisīn, what am I to do?'

Oisīn said, 'My heart is heavy to be saying it, but no man may break the bonds of geise. Break your faith with my father, but beware of his vengeance afterwards.'

And Dearmid turned to Osca, Oisīn's son, for young as he was, his counsel as well as his weapon-skill was well worth having.

'It is a sorry champion who breaks his geise, and the shadow of a man he will be afterwards.'

'Keelta Mac Ronan, what counsel do you give me?'

'Follow the Princess,' Keelta said, 'for indeed she would make an ill wife for Finn. But run swiftly and do not be checking to look back.'

Last of all, Dearmid turned to Dering, his closest friend and sworn sword brother.

'If you go with the Princess Grania,' Dering said (and they knew by his face that a flash of the Sight was on him), 'your death will come of it. Yet the man who breaks such a geise is not worthy to have lived at all.'

So Dearmid rose, and took his sword from where it hung behind him, and slung it on. He took his leave of the men who had been his friends since he came to manhood, knowing that he would never hunt with them nor sit at supper, nor fight at shoulder's touch with them ever again. All that was ended, because of Grania. He went out to the wicket gate.

Outside the gate, Grania was waiting with a dark cloak thrown about her. 'Go back,' he said. 'No one yet knows what has passed, save for a few who are my friends and will not speak of it. Go back and there's no one else will ever know.'

But Grania said, 'I will not go back. I will go with you because you have my heart in your breast.'

So Dearmid gave up the struggle, and said, 'If you will have it so, then I will have it so, and no man shall take you from me.'

They went westward and westward until they reached the Shannon ford, and there Dearmid took Grania up in his arms and carried her across, so that not the sole of her foot nor the trailing hem of her mantle were wetted. They went upstream a mile, and then turned southwest till they came to the Wood of the Two Tents. And in the thick heart of the Wood, Dearmid cut green branches with his sword and wove them into a cabin for Grania. And while she rested there, he brought her water from a nearby spring in his war-cap, and hunted for her so that she might eat and drink.

Early next morning, the King and his household and

his guests roused from their sleep, and found Dearmid and Grania flown. Then wild jealousy seized on Finn, and he sent for his trackers, men of the Clan Navan, and bade them follow on Dearmid's track.

The Clan Navan men followed the trail to the Shannon ford and up river to the place where Dearmid and Grania had turned southwest. Then they smelled the ground and took note of a grass blade lying over, and found a single strand of dark wool on a briar spray, and said to Finn, 'Easy enough now, for the trail runs straight towards the Wood of the Two Tents.'

So Finn bade the trackers go ahead while he and the rest of the Fianna followed on behind. And the trackers pushed forward, running low like hounds on the trail, until they came to the Wood and the thickest part of the Wood, and there they found a fenced enclosure. For Dearmid had cleared a space round his hut, and surrounded it by a stockade that no man could pierce. And seven narrow sapling-woven doors it had, facing seven different ways into the Wood.

One of the trackers climbed a tree from which he could look into the enclosure, and then went back and told Finn halted at the edge of the Wood that there was a fenced enclosure in the thick of the trees, and that Dearmid O'Dyna was inside it, with a woman whose hair was as dark as his own.

'That will be Grania, sure enough,' Finn said grimly, and ordered his men forward. So they came back to the heart of the Wood and the enclosure, and spread out to surround it. And within the stockade, Grania heard what was going forward, and trembled and fell to wild and silent weeping. And Dearmid kissed her three times and promised her that she need

have no fear, for all would yet be well with
them.

Now Angus Ōg, the most wise and fair and skilled
in magic of the Danann lords, was Dearmid's foster-
father, as has been told before, and loved him like a
son. And he knew by his magic art that Dearmid was
in deadly peril. And he came from the Boyne,
speeding on the wings of the south wind, with his
crown of wild swans flying about his head, and was
suddenly in the enclosure in the midst of the Wood of
the Two Tents.

Dearmid's heart leapt up at the sight of his foster-
father, and he would have flung his arms about him,
but Angus said only, 'What is this that you have done,
fosterling?'

And Dearmid told him all the story in as few words
as might be, with the Fianna moving outside the
stockade.

When he had finished, Angus Ōg, said, 'It is an ill
story, and I'm thinking it will have an ill end, but not
yet. Let the two of you come under my mantle, and
take each a corner of it, and I will bring you out from
this place, no man knowing.'

But Dearmid shook his head. 'Take Grania under
your mantle, but for me, I will find my own way out
and follow you. But if I should be killed, take the
Princess back to her father, and bid him to treat her
neither better nor worse for having chosen me.'

So Angus flung his mantle over Grania, his mantle
that was blue as the summer sky or the flowers of the
blue-eyed grass, and telling Dearmid where to follow,
leapt up once more invisible into the wind.

When they were gone, Dearmid took his sharp

spears in his hands and went to the nearest of the seven doors, and demanded to know who was outside it.

'Oisín and Osca,' came the answer, 'and with us none but Clan Bascna. Come out to us and none will harm you.'

'I will not come out to bring trouble upon you for your friendship to me,' said Dearmid, and he went and asked the same question at the second door.

'Keelta Mac Ronan and the Clan Ronan. Come out this way, and find none but friends.'

'It is not I that will bring trouble on the heads of my friends,' said Dearmid, and went to the third door.

'Conan of the Grey Rushes, and Fertai the son of Goll Mac Morna, and the Clan Morna. None of us best of friends with Finn, though we serve under his banner.'

And Dearmid went to the fourth door.

'A close comrade of yours is here, Guan of the Munster Fianna. We are from the same hunting runs, you and I and if need be I and my men will fight to the death for you.'

And Dearmid went to the fifth door.

'Finn the son of Glore Loud-Voice, and with me the Ulstermen. Come out to us, and we will kill you if we catch you, but we will take care not to see you pass.'

And Dearmid went to the sixth door.

'Clan Navan, watching for you like dogs at a rat hole. We are Finn's men. Come out to us and be a mark for our spears.'

'My spears are for warriors. I do not foul them with the blood of shoeless, trail-sniffing vagabonds!' And he went to the seventh door and demanded, 'Who stands outside?'

'Finn the son of Cool the son of Trenmor O'Bascna; and with me the Leinster Fianna,' came back the voice of Finn himself. 'Open the door and come out to me now, and we will carve your flesh from your sinews and your sinews from your bones.'

'This is my chosen door!' cried Dearmid. And he bent himself on to his spears and sprang aloft in a mighty hero's leap, out over the stockade and over the waiting warriors beyond, and with another bound was beyond reach of their weapons while they were still too shaken with surprise to follow.

Then he sped away southward, never halting until he reached the Wood of the Two Sallows, near Limerick.

And there he found Angus and Grania in a warm hut, roasting a wild boar on hazel spits over a blazing fire. Grania sprang up with a cry of joy when he appeared, and ran to fling her arms about him and draw him to the fire. So they ate their fill, and slept in peace until morning. Then Angus rose with the green dawn full of birdsong, and took his leave of them. 'Finn will never be turned aside from his vengeance,' said he, 'for he grows old, and it is bitter for an old man to lose his bride to a young one. Therefore remember this advice which I leave you. Go not into a tree with only one trunk, nor into a cave with only one opening. Where you cook your food, do not bide to eat it in the same place, and where you eat, do not bide to sleep. And where you sleep tonight, do not sleep tomorrow night.'

When Angus was gone, Dearmid and Grania went on westward till they reached the Stream of the Champions. Here they rested, and Dearmid speared a salmon, and built a fire on the near bank and fixed the salmon on hazel rods to broil. And when it was cooked, he carried both it and Grania across to the further bank before they ate. And when the meal was done, they moved further west before lying down to sleep, for they remembered the warning of Angus Ōg.

So they went on, moving always about and about the country, and never settling half a day in one place lest Finn should come up with them, until at last they came to the Forest of Dooros in the district of Hi Ficna in Sligo, which was guarded by a giant named Sharvan the Surly.

Now this is how Sharvan the Surly came to have the Forest of Dooros under his guardianship.

Once, the Dananns and the Fianna played a game of hurley together among the lakes of Killarney. They played for three days and three nights, and neither could win a single goal from the other. And at the end of that time, the Dananns, finding that they could not overcome the Fianna, abandoned the game and went northward in a body.

The Dananns had for food during the game and the journey, crimson nuts and arbutus apples and scarlet quicken berries, which they had brought with them from the Land of Promise. These were magic, and the Dananns took great care that no nut nor apple nor berry should touch the mortal soil of Erin. But as they were going through the Forest of Dooros, a single scarlet quicken berry fell to the ground unnoticed.

From this berry grew a mighty quicken tree, and it with as much magic to it as ever there was to a quicken tree of Fairyland, for the berries tasted like honey, and if a man were a hundred and sixty years old, he had only to eat three of the berries to return to his prime.

When the Dananns found what had happened, they sent a giant of their own people, Sharvan the Surly, to keep guard on it so that no mortal man should eat the magic berries.

Sharvan made a powerful protector for the tree; he was huge and strong and very ugly with only one eye, and that a fiery red one in the middle of his forehead. And he was so skilled in magic arts fire could not burn him, water could not drown him and weapon could not wound him. Indeed the only way he could be killed at all was by three blows with his own iron-bound club. All day he sat at the foot of the tree, and at night he slept in a hut high in its branches.

In this land, Dearmid knew that he and Grania might be safe from Finn, for Sharvan allowed no one, especially the Fianna, to hunt in the Forest of Dooros. So leaving Grania in hiding at a safe distance, he went boldly to Sharvan sitting at the foot of the quicken tree, and asked his leave to live in Dooros, and hunt there for himself and his woman.

The giant turned his one red eye on him, and answered shortly and harshly that he might live and hunt where he pleased so long as he never made a single move to touch a single berry of the quicken tree.

So Dearmid built a hunting bothie, and set up a stockade round it, and there for a while he and Grania lived in peace and safety.

Finn did not abandon his pursuit of them, but he let it lie for a while, and went back to his own place, to Almu of the White Walls.

And there came to him one day two splendid-seeming young warriors, who bowed low before him, and when he asked what brought them to Almu, the eldest said, 'I am Angus the son of Art Mac Morna, and here beside me is Aedh the son of Andala Mac Morna. Our fathers fought against yours in the battle of Cnucha, for which, later, you slew them and outlawed us their sons, which was scarcely just, seeing that our fathers were but boys in the fighting-time, and *we* were not born until many years after the battle. But now we have come to ask that you make peace with us and give us our fathers' places in the ranks of the Fianna.'

'That I will do', said Finn, 'but first you shall pay me the death-fine for *my* father.'

'Gladly would we pay, if we could,' said the young men, 'but we have neither gold nor silver nor cattle.'

And Finn said, 'The fine that I ask is not of gold, or silver, or cattle.'

'Of what, then, great Captain?'

'I ask only one of two things. The head of Dearmid O'Dyna, or a handful of berries from the Fairy quicken tree that grows in the Forest of Dooros!'

'I have good counsel for you,' said Oisīn, standing by his father's side, and he spoke kindly. 'Go back to the place you came from, and forget that ever you came seeking peace with Finn Mac Cool and places in the Fianna.'

'We would rather die in seeking this death-fine which the Fian Lord demands, than go back to the place we came from, defeated before even making the trial.'

So they set out. They found the Wood of the Two Sallows, and from there they followed the trail to the

Forest of Dooros, and so came at last to the hunting bothie.

Dearmid, inside with Grania, heard their voices, and snatching up his spear, went to the door and demanded who was there.

'We are Angus son of Art Mac Morna, and Aedh the son of Andala Mac Morna. And we come from Almu of the White Walls to get for Finn Mac Cool the head of Dearmid O'Dyna, or a handful of berries from the quicken tree of Dooros, for that is the death-fine he demands of us because our fathers had a hand in the slaying of *his* father.'

Dearmid laughed, but somewhat grimly. 'Alas! I am Dearmid O'Dyna, and I'll not be giving you my head, for I've a use for it myself. And as for the berries, they will be as hard to come by as my head, for you will have to fight the giant Sharvan for them, he who can neither be burned in the fire nor drowned with water nor wounded with blade. But since you must be taking one or the other, which will you try for first?'

'We will try first for your head.'

So they made ready for the fight. They agreed to fight with their bare hands, and laid aside their weapons. And they agreed that if the Sons of Clan Morna were the winners, they should have Dearmid's head to take back to Finn, and if Dearmid won, he should have their heads to hang on the roof beam of his bothie.

They then set to, but the fight was a short one, and though Dearmid took them both together, they were soon overcome and at his mercy.

Now, for a long while past, Grania had been filled

with longing to taste the magic quicken berries, and until this day she had not spoken of her craving, for she knew the trouble that would come of it if she did. But when the fight was over, and the two young men bound and helpless, she told Dearmid how much she longed for the berries. And, 'Three of you might succeed in overcoming the giant, where one could not,' she said.

'You do not know what you ask,' Dearmid told her, standing over his captives. 'Our sanctuary here depends on the friendship of Sharvan, and if I steal for you these berries that it is his life to guard, it will surely be the death of both of us!'

'Indeed I do know, and so I have fought against my longing,' Grania said. 'Yet it grows greater day by day, and I think that if I do not taste the berries, I shall die in any case.'

Dearmid was filled with grief and foreboding, but stronger than these was his fear that harm would come to Grania if she did not get the berries. So at last he said, 'Well enough, then; I will get you the berries, but I will be going alone for them.'

But when the two young men heard this, they cried out from the ground, 'Unbind us, and we will go with you!'

'It is little enough help that you would be to me,' Dearmid said, 'and in any case, this that I go on is *my* fight.'

'Then let us come and stand by to watch,' pleaded the young men, 'for surely this will be fighting such as we have not seen before!'

And in the end Dearmid agreed, and unbound them, and went to the quicken tree with the two following close behind him. He found the giant sleeping, and roused him by a blow with the flat of his sword.

Sharvan glared up at him with his one red eye. 'What is it you want, that you cannot let me sleep?'

'The Princess Grania my wife longs for a taste of the quicken berries from the tree you guard. And if she does not get them, assuredly she will die. Therefore I pray you give me a few berries to save her life.'

'Not one berry, not if she lay before me dying at this moment,' growled the giant.

Dearmid moved a step nearer and drew his sword. 'Because you have dealt fairly by us, I have awakened you to ask for the berries, instead of stealing them while you slept. But before I leave this place, I will have them, whether you will or no.'

Then the giant sprang up and seized his club and aimed three mighty blows at Dearmid, which he only just managed to turn on his upflung shield. But he knew that Sharvan expected him to attack with his sword, and so he flung it aside, and the shield with it, and leaping in beneath the giant's guard, twisted his arms about the huge body, and heaving with all his might, flung him over his shoulder and crashing to the ground. Then he seized the giant's great iron club and with it dealt him three mighty blows that drove the life out of him like the wind from a goatskin bellows.

Dearmid sat down, far spent and sore at heart, and when the Sons of Morna came up, loud with rejoicing, bade them drag the giant aside into the thick of the trees, and bury him.

Then Grania also came, and Dearmid reached up and picked the glowing berry-clusters for her until she had eaten her fill. Then he picked more clusters and gave them to the Sons of Morna, saying, 'Take these to Finn, and tell him that it was you who slew the giant Sharvan.'

'Our thanks to you, Dearmid O'Dyna,' said Angus. 'We could never have got for ourselves the berries to pay the death-fine, and though our heads are forfeit to you, you have most generously left them on our shoulders.'

And so they went their way.

But Dearmid and Grania, now that Sharvan was dead, and their safety lost to them, left the hunting bothie and lived in the hut which the giant had built among the branches of the quicken tree, where they were completely hidden from the ground.

The two young warriors came back to Almu of the White Walls, and stood before Finn with the bright berries in their hands, and told him, 'Sharvan the giant is dead, and here are the berries from the quicken tree of Dooros, the agreed death-fine for your father Cool.'

Finn took the berries and smelled them three times. 'These are indeed the berries of the magic quicken tree; but they have been in the hands of Dearmid O'Dyna, for I smell his touch on them. It was Dearmid, not you, who slew Sharvan and gathered these berries.' His voice grew cold and terrible. 'You did not get my father's death-fine by your own strength and cunning, and you made friendship between yourselves and my sorest enemy. No peace do you get from me, nor a place among the Fianna!'

Then he called together the Leinster Fianna, and marched into Hi Ficna, to the Forest of Dooros. The trackers found Dearmid's trail to the foot of the quicken tree, and they found the magic berries unguarded, and ate their fill from the lower branches.

'We have marched long and the day is hot,' said Finn. 'I will rest a while here in the shade, for well I know that Dearmid is somewhere in the branches over our heads and cannot be escaping us while we keep the tree surrounded.'

'Surely you are crazed with jealousy, my father,' Oisīn protested, 'if you think that Dearmid has waited for you, knowing that you must trail him here!'

But Finn took no notice, and called for a chess board and bade Oisīn play with him. They played until the game reached a point at which Oisīn thought that he was beaten. But Finn said, 'You could win this game with one move, Oisīn my son, but I challenge you to find what move it is.'

And Oisīn frowned at the board and could not see any move that would help him.

Then Dearmid, who had been watching the game through the branches from his hiding place above, thought to himself, 'Many times have you helped me, Oisīn my sword-brother, and shall I not be helping you now?' And he plucked a single berry, and tossed it down with such skilful aim that it struck one of Oisīn's chessmen, and bounced off to a certain square of the board. And Oisīn moved that piece to the square where the quicken berry lay as bright as a bead of red coral, and with that move, he won the game.

And they played a second time, and again they reached a point at which Oisīn could win the game with one move, and only one, and could not for the life of him see what the move should be. And again Dearmid dropped a berry that struck one of the

chessmen and flicked off on to a certain square of the
board. And again Oisīn moved that piece to the square
where the quicken berry lay red as a hot spark — and
won the game.

And a third time they played, and reached the same
pass; and a third time Dearmid dropped a quicken
berry, that struck and bounced off one of the pieces,
and Oisīn moved that piece to the square where the
fallen berry lay red as a drop of blood, and won that
game also.

'You have become a better chess player than you
used to be,' said Finn, 'as good as Dearmid O'Dyna
— or is it that Dearmid is guiding you from the
branches above us?' And he flung back his angry head
and shouted, 'Are you there, then, Dearmid O'Dyna?'

And Dearmid answered, for it was against his
honour to keep silence when his old Captain asked
direct. 'I am here, Finn Mac Cool, and with me the
Princess Grania, my wife.'

And looking up they all saw him plainly, looking
down at them through a gap in the leafy branches.

Then Grania, understanding their deadly danger,
began to tremble and weep. And indeed she had good
cause, for Finn now ordered his warriors to surround
the tree in a circle and another circle outside that and
another outside again, and so on until there was a
broad band many warriors deep all about the quicken
tree, hand-linked so as to leave no gap through which
a hare could have escaped. And he offered fine body
armour and weapons and a higher place than he
already held in the Fianna to any man who would
climb the tree and bring down the head of Dearmid
O'Dyna.

Up sprang Garva of Slieve Cua. 'I am your man! Dearmid's father slew my father, and now it is the time for vengeance!' And he began to climb the tree.

Now at that instant the knowledge came to Angus Ōg at Brugh-Na-Boyna that his foster-son was in deadly peril. And he spread his cloak and took the wings of the autumn wind, and the Fianna on guard about the quicken tree saw no more than a shadow as of wild swans flying overhead; but Dearmid and Grania saw to their joy and relief the tall Danann chieftain standing between them.

And as Garva, climbing from branch to branch, drew near, Dearmid struck out at him with his foot and sent him crashing to the ground. And Angus Ōg put the likeness of Dearmid upon him even as he fell, and the Fianna struck his head off almost before he reached the ground.

But a moment later a cry of grief and rage rose from them, as the body resumed its true likeness, and they knew who it was they had slain.

Then another champion came forward to climb the tree, and another and another. And each of them Dearmid and Angus dealt with in the same way, until nine headless bodies lay at the foot of the quicken tree, and Finn was half mad with grief and rage.

Then Angus said that the thing had gone on long enough, and he would take them out of that place of danger. But Dearmid replied much as he had done in the Wood of the Two Tents. 'Let you take Grania. But as for me, I'll fight my own way out.' Then he kissed Grania tenderly, and said, 'If I live till evening, I will follow you. And if not, then Angus my foster-father shall take you safe back to Tara.'

And Angus Ōg flung his cloak over Grania, and was gone, the Fianna seeing nothing but a moment of beating of wild swan's wings against the sky, and so bore her off to the safety of Brugh-Na-Boyna.

Left alone, Dearmid took up his spears and shouted to Finn, 'Never was the Fianna in danger, that I did not share it. When we went to battle I went first, but came last when we left the field. But I see now that you will never turn from this hunting trail until I am slain. And why should I fear death more, now, than on some later day? Therefore I am coming down to you out of this tree; but it is fair warning I'm giving you, that I shall slay as many of the Fianna as I can lay blade to — aye, or my naked hands for that matter — before they pull me down to my death. So now, have my life if you will — and pay for it dearly with the lives of your men.'

Then young Osca spoke up. 'Finn, my grandfather, Dearmid speaks truly of the perils he shared with you and all of us, and of his place in battle. Give him forgiveness for the ill doing that was forced upon him, for already he has suffered much.'

'My peace and forgiveness be upon Dearmid when I have his head,' said Finn.

'Then I, Osca, take his safety upon myself. And if any man harm Dearmid O'Dyna while he has the shelter of my shield, may the green earth open and swallow me, may the grey seas roll in and overwhelm me, may the stars of the sky fall upon me all together and crush me out of life with their weight of brightness.' And looking up into the tree he shouted, 'Come down, Dearmid, and we will fight our way out of this together.'

But Dearmid chose the side of the tree where the men stood closest to the trunk, and walked out, hidden by the leaves and bright berry-clusters, along a thick branch, until it began to dip and sway beneath him. Then he sprang out and down, beyond the outermost circle of the waiting warriors, and leapt forward and away at such speed that in three heartbeats of time he was beyond range of their spears. And in seven heartbeats Osca was racing beside him; Osca looking back once at the Leinster Fianna with such a face that not one man dare to come after them.

So the two heroes held on their way until they came at last to Brugh-Na-Boyna and found Angus and Grania waiting for them.

As for Finn, sick with rage, he went back to the Hill of Almu, and bade his best and swiftest war-boat to be made ready and provisioned for a long voyage.

And when all was done as he had ordered, he went on board, and nothing more is known of him until he came to the Land of Promise, where his two foster-mothers now lived. He went to the one of them who had been a Druidess and possessed the Wise Craft, which folk call witchcraft nowadays, and told her all that had passed, and begged her help. 'For,' said he, 'it is beyond the strength and cunning of men to slay this Dearmid. Nothing save magic can touch him.'

'Whatever you wish done, I will do, and whoever you wish harmed, I will harm, for your sake,' said the Witch-Woman. 'For are you not my fosterling? And do I not love you better than ever woman loved child of her own?'

And next day she returned with him to Erin, to

Brugh-Na-Boyna, and no man saw them come, for she flung about them a magic mist, such as the Druid-kind were used to weave.

It chanced, that day, that Dearmid hunted in the woods alone, for Osca, having companied with him till he was in seeming safety, had returned to his place among the Fian chiefs. And when the Witch-Woman knew this she took a water-lily leaf and made a singing magic over it, so that it became a broad flat millstone with a hole in the centre. And seating herself on this, she rose into the air, floating over the treetops until she came directly over where Dearmid was. Then, standing up on the millstone, she began to aim poisoned darts at him through the hole in the middle of it. The darts pierced Dearmid's hunting leathers and his light shield as though they had been made of rotten birch bark, and each dart carried in its barbed point the sting of a hundred angry hornets, so that Dearmid in his agony, knew that unless he could slay the witch, and quickly, he must surely die. Then he seized the Ga-Derg, his great spear, and leaning far back, launched it upward with such deadly aim that it passed through the hole in the millstone and through the Witch-Woman's body as she leaned forward to hurl another dart, and with a shriek, she fell dead at his feet.

And he twisted one hand in her long tangled grey hair, and struck off her head, and took it back to Brugh-Na-Boyna, and told Angus and Grania what had passed.

Then Angus judged that the time had come at last, when Finn Mac Cool might be ready to make peace. And the next morning he rose and went to the Fian

Captain on the Hill of Almu and asked him if he would not now bury the feud.

And Finn, seeing that even witchcraft seemed unable to slay Dearmid, and that the quarrel had cost the lives of many of his men, and now even the life of his foster-mother, felt suddenly old and weary, and agreed to make peace.

Then Angus went to Tara, to Cormac Mac Art, and asked if he too would give Dearmid peace and pardon for taking the Princess Grania. And Cormac pulled his beard and said that it was hard to make peace with the man who had carried off the daughter of his house from her rightfully betrothed husband but none the less, he would do it, if Cairbri his son who would be King after him, was of the same mind.

And Cairbri, who already hated Finn in his heart for his power in the land, and had been angry with a deep and secret anger, that his sister should be given in marriage to the Fian Captain and so increase his power, said, 'The quarrel was never mine, and I had sooner have one Dearmid than twenty Finn Mac Cools for marriage-kin. I give neither peace nor pardon, for I never broke the one, and I see no need of the other. Tell Dearmid that I am no more and no less his friend than I always have been.'

So Angus Ōg went back to Dearmid his foster-son and said, 'Peace is better than war. Will you now have peace from Finn Mac Cool and from Cormac the High King, and believe that Cairbri who will be High King after him is no more and no less your friend than he always has been?'

'Gladly will I do so!' said Dearmid. 'But let them

grant me conditions that befit a champion of the Fianna and the husband of the Princess Grania.'

'And what conditions are those?'

'The lands that were my father's — the Holding of O'Dyna without rent or tribute to King or High King, and the Holding of Ben Damis in Leinster. These from Finn, and neither he nor the Fianna shall hunt over them without my leave. And from the High King, the Holding of Kesh-Carron as a dowry for his daughter.'

Finn and Cormac both agreed; and so the peace was made between them.

So Dearmid and Grania built themselves a home in Kesh-Carron, far from the places where the kings and heroes gathered. And there they lived happily enough, and Grania bore four sons to Dearmid. And Dearmid grew rich in cattle, and all went well with them for many years.

12
Niamh of the Golden Hair

One day Finn and Oisīn and a small company of the
Fianna rode hunting among the lakes of Killarney.
There were new faces among Finn's hunting
companions, and some of the old ones lacking. Goll
Mac Morna, his faithful friend ever since that morning
on the ramparts of Tara, when he had accepted the new
Fian Captain, had died the winter before, and Finn
missed the grim old one-eyed champion so that even
the joys of the hunt seemed a littled dulled because
Goll was not hunting beside him.

But the early summer morning was as fair as a
morning of the Land of Youth, the dew lying grey on
the grass, save where the rising sun made rainbows in
it; the thorn trees curdled white with honey-scented
blossom, and the small birds singing to draw the heart
out of the breast. The deer fled from the thickets and
the hounds followed them in full cry, their trail-music
at last stirring even Finn's heart to gladness.

But they had not long been at their hunting, when
they saw a horse and rider coming towards them from
the West, and as they drew nearer, the waiting Fianna
saw before them a maiden mounted on a white steed.
She drew rein as she came up with them, and the
whole hunting party stood amazed. For never before
had any of them seen a sight so lovely. Her yellow hair
was bound back by a slender golden diadem from a

forehead as white as windflowers; her eyes were blue as the morning sky and clear as the dew sparkling on the fern fronds. Her mantle was of brown silk scattered with a skyful of golden stars, and fell from her shoulders to brush the ground. Her white horse was shod with pure yellow gold, his proud neck arching as a wave in the instant before it breaks; and she sat him more gracefully than a white swan on the waters of Killarney.

Finn broke the silence at last, bending his head before her in all courtesy. 'Beautiful Princess — for surely it is a princess you are — will you tell me your name and where you come from?'

And she answered in a voice as sweet as the chiming of small crystal bells, 'Finn Mac Cool, Captain of the Fianna of Erin, my country lies far off in the wester sea. I am the daugher of the King of Tyr-na-nOg, and I am called Niamh of the Golden Hair.'

'And what is it that brings you to the land of Erin, so far from your home?'

'My love for your son, Oisīn,' said the maiden. 'So often and so often have I heard of his grace and goodliness, his gentleness and valour, that my heart learned to love him, and for his sake I have refused all the chiefs and princes who have come seeking me in marriage; and for his sake now, I have come on this far journey from Tyr-na-nOg.'

Then turning to where Oisīn stood close by, holding out her hands, she said, 'Come with me to Tyr-na-nOg, the Land of the Ever Young. The trees of my land bear fruit and blossom and green leaves together all the year round, and sorrow and pain and age are unknown. You shall have a hundred silken robes each differently worked with gold, and a hundred swift-pacing steeds, and a hundred slender keen-scenting hounds. You shall have herds of cattle without number, and flocks of sheep with fleeces of gold; a coat of mail, you shall have, that no weapon ever pierced and a sword that never missed its mark. A hundred warriors shall follow you at your call, a hundred harpers delight you with sweet music. And I will be your true and ever-loving wife, if you will come with me to Tyr-na-nOg.'

Oisĩn drew near and took her hands, and stood looking up at her out of those strange dark eyes of his that he had from his mother. 'Keep all these things you promise me, save only for the last. If you will be my true and loving wife, I will come with you, further than to Tyr-na-nOg.'

The Fianna looked to each other and back again to Oisĩn. They protested in anger and grief, and Finn went forward and set his huge warrior's hand on his son's shoulder and turned him so that he must look at him and away from Niamh of the Golden Hair. 'Oisĩn my son, do not go! If you wish for a wife, are there not women fair enough in Erin?'

'She is my choice, before all the women of all the Worlds,' said Oisĩn.

And Finn saw that the Fairy blood that was in him from his mother was stronger now than the blood of mortal men, and that because of it, he would go where Niamh called.

'Then go,' he said, 'for nothing that I can say, nor the voice of your son, nor the music of your hounds can hold you, that I know. And oh, Oisĩn, my heart is heavy, for I shall never see you again.'

'I shall come back,' said Oisīn, 'surely I shall come back before long, and I shall come back often.' And he flung his arms about his father's shoulders and strained him close, then went from one to another of his friends, taking his leave of them all. Only Dearmid O'Dyna was not there for his leave-taking. Lastly he bade farewell to Osca his son, while all the while the maiden sat her white horse, waiting.

Then he mounted behind her, and she shook the bridle and the white horse broke forward into a gallop as swift as the west wind and as smooth as silk, his four golden shoes seeming scarcely to bend the grasses beneath his hooves, until he reached the seashore. And his golden shoes left no mark on the white sand. And when he came to the edge of the waves, he neighed three times, and shook his head so that his mane flew like spray. Then he sprang forward, skimming over the waves with the speed of a homing swallow. And the distance closed in behind him and the two on his back, so that those who watched from the green land saw them no more.

Now this, that I have told you, is not yet the story of Oisín but only the beginning of the story; for the end of it belongs to a later time.

The end of it is the end of all this long and strange and tangled tale of Finn Mac Cool and the Fianna of Erin.

13
The Death of Dearmid

The years went by and the years went by, and in Dearmid's house in Kesh-Carron, Grania said to Dearmid one day, 'Seeing the greatness of our household and the size of our herds and the number of our folk, is it fitting that we should live so cut off from the world? Is it fitting, especially, that the greatest man in all Erin, after the High King, my father, Finn Mac Cool the Captain of his Fianna, has never eaten salt nor drunk wine beneath our roof?'

'You should be knowing the answer to that,' said Dearmid. 'There is cold-peace between Finn and me, but no man could say that there was friendship. That is why we live far off and to ourselves, and why he has not set foot across our threshold.'

But Grania protested. 'Surely after all these years the old quarrel is dead and over. Now, let us bid him to a great feast, and try to win his full friendship back to us.'

And much against his will, Dearmid yielded, as he always yielded to her wishes in the end.

So they prepared a great feast, and when all was ready they sent to invite Finn Mac Cool with the chiefs and champions of the Fianna.

And Finn came, and with him his household and companions and their horses and dogs. And they spent many days under the roof of Dearmid O'Dyna, hunting and feasting.

Only one quarry they never hunted, and that was the wild boar, for Dearmid was under geise never to hunt boar.

The reason for that geise was a strange one indeed, and this was the way of it.

It had been told before, how Dearmid was reared at Brugh-Na-Boyna, as foster-son to Angus Ōg. Well, now, Angus had a steward, and Dearmid's mother, who had not always been faithful to her own lord, his father, had borne this steward a son. And when Dearmid's father sent him to Brugh-Na-Boyna for fostering, the steward's son was fostered with him, so that he might have a companion and not be lonely. This boy, of course, was his half-brother as well as his foster-kin, because both had the same mother, though one was the son of the chieftain Donn O'Dyna, and the other the son of Angus Ōg's steward.

One day Donn came with a few others of the Fianna to visit Angus Ōg and see how his son was doing. That evening as they sat at supper, a fight broke out among the hounds in the hall, and the women and children scattered, squealing, while the men waded in to stop the fight. In the confusion the steward's son chanced to run for shelter between Donn's knees. Hatred flashed up in Donn, remembering who was the boy's mother, and he shut his knees so fiercely that he killed the child on the spot. Then he threw the little body under the feet of the hounds, no one seeing what had happened.

When the fighting hounds were parted, the boy's

body was discovered, and the steward snatched it up, crying with grief and fury that the hounds had slain his son. But among the hunting party was Finn Mac Cool himself (he was young then, and newly come to be Captain of the Fianna) and he bade the steward to look for the child's injuries, and when they looked, there was no scratch nor tooth mark to be found on him, only the bruises on his crushed sides. Then the steward guessed what had happened, and demanded that the boy Dearmid should be placed between *his* knees, to do with as he would.

Angus Ōg was red-angry at this, and Donn would have struck off the steward's head, if Finn had not come between them.

The steward said nothing more, but left the hall and returned carrying in his hand a hazel wand. With this he struck the body of his son, and instantly in place of the dead child, there sprang up a huge wild boar. A black boar without ears or tail!

Then, holding out the hazel wand, he chanted over the great beast this spell:

'By the Power of this Wand
Listen and obey.
This I put upon you,
This I put on Dearmid,
You who shared one mother,
   Share one fate henceforth.
Share one span of life,
Share one death at last,
Brother slaying brother,
Death-fine for each other
   On that fatal day.

And as he spoke the last words, the boar rushed through the open door to the hall, and disappeared into the night.

And in the silent and horror-stricken hall, Angus took up the remaining child on his knees, and laid on him the most solemn geise that he should never hunt wild boar, both because of the kinship between him and the black boar, and because so, and only so, was there a hope that he might escape the doom laid on him by the steward in vengeance for his own son.

So it was that during the days that Finn and his companions spent as Dearmid's guests, there was hunting of wolf and badger and red deer, but never of wild boar.

And then one night, long after all men were in bed and asleep, Dearmid roused to hear the distant yelping of a hound on a hot scent, and he started up on one elbow, listening, with a strange sense of dread. But his sudden movement roused Grania, and she started up also, and flung her arms round him, and asked what was amiss.

'I heard a hound baying on the scent,' Dearmid said, 'and surely that is a strange thing to be hearing at midnight!'

'May all things guard you from harm!' said Grania quickly, and made the sign with her fingers to turn aside ill luck. 'It was one of the courtyard dogs hunting in his sleep. Now lie down again.'

Dearmid lay down and slept. But again he was roused by the belling of a hound, and started up and reached for his cloak to go and look to the matter. But again, Grania held him back. 'If it was not one of our dogs, then at this hour it can only have been a hound of the Fairy Kind; and it is not good to see the milk-white hounds at their hunting. Lie down again, dear love.'

And Dearmid lay down again and slept deep and long; but with the first grey glimmer of daylight stealing in through the open door, the voice of the hound roused him a third time.

And a third time Grania would have held him back, but he stood up, despite her clinging, and reached for his cloak and flung it round him, laughing. 'See, the daylight is growing, and the white hounds of the Danann do not hunt once the sun is above the hills. This is some lost hound, hunting on his own account, and I will go and bring him in.'

Grania had a dark dread on her, and she not knowing why, and she said, 'If you will go, then take with you the Ga-Derg, your great spear that Angus gave you, for the hairs rise on the back of my neck and I smell danger.'

But Dearmid still laughed. 'How can there be danger in the trail-music of a single hound? The Ga-Derg is a war spear. I will take the Ga-boi, my light spear, if that will make you happy. And my good hound Mac-an-Choill shall go with me.'

And whistling Mac-an-Choill to heel, he started out in the direction from which he had heard the baying of the strange hound. And as he went, he heard the hound again, and others with him now, and knew that this was no stray after all, but the hunting of a whole pack. He pressed on, the sounds of the hunt seeming sometimes nearer and sometimes further away, until he came to Ben Bulben, and climbed its steep grassy sides, and on the round crest of Ben Bulben he found Finn, quite alone.

Dearmid was angry that men were hunting his hills without his leave, and he gave Finn no very courteous greeting, but, still panting from his climb, demanded to know who it was that had unleashed the hounds.

'Some of our men took the hounds out at midnight, being restless and hot-headed from drinking wine,' Finn said. 'One of the hounds found the scent of a wild boar. Indeed I would have stopped the chase if I had but been here in time, for I know this trail they follow, the trail of the Wild Boar of Ben Bulben, and to go after that one is a far worse danger to the hunter than to the hunted. Many good men and hounds have died on his tushes before today.' Suddenly as he spoke, his eyes widened and he pointed into the distance behind Dearmid. 'And see, the thing happens again − the Boar has broken cover and our men are running from him! It is *he* that is hunting *them!*'

And turning to look where the old Fian captain pointed, Dearmid saw that what he said was true.

For a few moments they watched in horror, then Finn cried out, 'He is heading uphill − making towards this very spot! It is in my mind that the sooner we are out of his way, the better!'

'I will not move aside for a hunted boar!' Dearmid said, and his hand tightened on his spear.

'This is no mortal boar, and it is not *he* that is the hunted one! Remember also that you are under the geise never to hunt wild pig!'

And now it seemed that a madness seized upon Dearmid; but in truth it was the old doom working within him. And he shouted in defiance, 'Neither for fear of this boar, nor for any other wild beast, nor for the keeping of my geise unbroken, will I leave this place like a scared hound with my tail between my legs!'

So Finn went his way with a strange mingling of feelings within him, so that he wanted at one and the same time to fling his spear at the sky and laugh until his heart burst within his breast, and to lie with his face on the ground and howl like a dog over a dead master, for all the sorrows that ever had happened since the world began.

And Dearmid, left standing on the hill crest, alone save for his hound, looked after Finn Mac Cool, and said in his heart, 'Now, did you, my old Captain rouse, the Boar and set on this chase, hoping that my death would come of it? Well, if I am fated to die in this spot, then I am fated. No man may escape his doom.'

And he made ready to receive the Boar, as it came thundering up the mountain slope with the Fianna far-scattered all about it. As it came, Dearmid loosed Mac-an-Choill against it, but though till now the hound had always been the bravest of the brave, he turned and fled howling before the wicked red-eyed thing that had neither ears nor tail.

Then Dearmid set his finger in the silken loop of the Ga-boi and hurled the light spear with perfect aim. It struck the boar in the middle of the forehead, but fell to the ground without so much as disturbing one of the brute's harsh black bristles. Then, cursing himself that he had not heeded Grania's advice as to his weapons, he ripped his hunting-blade from its sheath and, with the brute right upon him, struck a mighty blow at the black neck behind where the ears should have been.

But the blade flew into a score of pieces, leaving only
the hilt in his hand; and not so much as one bristle of
the board's hide was cut through.

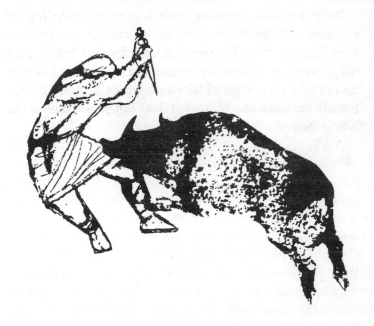

And now, as Dearmid, quite defenceless, leapt aside,
the great brute swung round upon him with a squeal
of fury and hurled him to the ground, and rooting for
for him, as a tame pig roots for acorns in the ground,
brought him up on the curve of its mighty tushes, and
flung him down once more with a ghastly wound torn
out of his side and pouring red into the grass.
Squealing still, it backed, and turned to charge again,
but Dearmid, with his last despairing strength, flung
the dagger hilt at him so mightily that it broke the flat
skull and drove through to the brain, and the Boar of

Ben Bulben crashed to the ground and rolled over dead.

Then Finn and the rest of the hunting band came up. And Finn stood looking down on Dearmid while he lay bleeding his life away, and said at last in a harsh and grating voice, 'Not so beautiful now, eh, my Dearmid of the Love Spot?'

And Dearmid gasped, 'It is in your power to heal me, even now, Finn Mac Cool.'

'How?' said Finn.

'All men know that you can heal even a man at the point of death.'

'True enough,' said Finn, 'but tell me, Dearmid O'Dyna, why should I be giving back life to you, of all the men in Erin?'

'In return for the times that I saved yours,' Dearmid answered, and groaned in his bitter pain and the sorrow of old friendship turned to hate. 'Do you remember the night we rested at the house of Derca Donnara, and even as we sat at the table, Cairbri of the Liffey with your enemies of Tara and of Bregia and of Mide, surrounded the place and threw firebrands into the thatch? And when you would have rushed forth to meet them, and doubtless also the death they had in their spears for you, *I* thrust you back into your seat and bade you finish the feast, and sallied out with my own men to quench the flames and drive back your enemies? For Cairbri was no enemy of *mine*! If I had asked you for a drink from your cupped hands that night, when we came back into the hall with our wounds red upon us, you would have given it to me gladly enough.'

'Then. But not now,' said Finn.

'Or the night that you were captive in the Hostel of the Quicken Trees, and I held the ford, that your enemies might not come upon you helpless, and afterwards brought up the bleeding heads of three kings in the hollow of my shield, to set you free? If I had asked you for a drink at that night's end, would you have refused me?'

'Not then. But now,' Finn said.

'Now! Even now! Give me a drink from your hands!' Dearmid begged weakly. 'For the chill of death creeps upon me; and I tell you this. I see a day — a day of slaughter and despair — and after it, few enough of the Fianna left to tell how it ended. Then you will need my help as never you needed it before, and bitter in your heart shall be the memory of this day on Ben Bulben, when you could have saved me and would not, and my place empty beside your shoulder, that might have been staunchly filled.'

Then Osca spoke up, kneeling with Dearmid's head on his knee, his voice soft and ugly in his throat. 'Finn my grandfather, an ill thing it is, that I should be speaking to you so, but speak I will, and it is you that shall listen! *You shall give Dearmid to drink from your cupped hands; and quickly, lest it be too late!*'

'Even if I would, there is no water to be had in this place.'

'That is not true,' Dearmid whispered, 'and you know it, my Captain, for not nine paces from here, hidden under that bramble bush, is a spring of clear water.'

So Finn went to the spring, and cupping his two hands together he brought up a palmful of water, and turned back to Dearmid. But midway, the memory of

Grania's choice rose in him again, and he let the precious water run through his fingers.

'Try again, Finn my grandfather,' said Osca, still more softly, and his black brows drew together.

And Finn stooped again and filled his cupped hands, and again turned back to Dearmid, and midway, remembered Grania, and let the water trickle through his fingers.

'Finn my grandfather,' said Osca, and his voice was softer than ever, 'near kin as we are, if you do not bring the water this third time, only one of us two shall leave Ben Bulben crest alive!'

And Finn saw that the young warrior meant it, and though indeed he knew that in single combat he could still slay Osca or any other of the Fianna, a cold horror woke in his belly, and he turned back a third time to the water, and came quickly, not a drop now spilling through his fingers, But even as he reached his side, Dearmid's head dropped back and the life went out of him on a long sigh.

The Fianna gathered about him, and set up three long heavy shouts for the death of Dearmid O'Dyna. And when they were silent, Osca laid Dearmid gently down on the stained and trampled grass, and said, looking straight and steady up at Finn, 'I wish that it was you were lying here in Dearmid's stead! For now the bravest and most generous heart in all the Fianna is still.' And he bent his head and wept. 'Why was I not remembering that Dearmid's life was linked with the life of a wild boar? I would have found some means to call off the hunt, and so delay for a while longer this time of sorrow!'

Then they left the hill, Finn leading the hound Mac-

an-Choill. But Osca and Dering and Mac Lugha
turned back and flung their cloaks over Dearmid's
body, before they followed the others.

Grania sat in the look-out place of her home,
watching for Dearmid's return. And at last she saw the
hunting party on the homeward track and Finn Mac
Cool walking foremost, leading Dearmid's great
hound. But of Dearmid himself, no sign, not so much
as his shadow on the grass. And then she understood
and fell all her length senseless on the ground, while
her women wailed about her.

When she came to herself once more, the hunting
party was within the gates, and the word running
through the household that Dearmid had got his death
from the Wild Boar of Ben Bulben. Then all the people
within the dun raised three loud and bitter cries of
lamentation which rang through the glens and across
the lonely moors and pierced the very clouds of the
sky. But Grania's wailing rose above them all.

When at last she became calm, she ordered her
people to go to Ben Bulben and fetch home the body
of her lord. Then she turned to Finn, who stood by,
still holding Mac-an-Choill in leash, and said, 'You
will be going from here, now, for this is no place
where you would wish to be. But leave me my lord's
hound.'

'Surely a hound can be little use to you,' said Finn,
'and a hunting dog will do better with a man than with
a woman.'

But Osca, as white as Dearmid lying dead on Ben
Bulben, came forward and took the leash from Finn's
hand and gave it to Grania.

When Grania's people came to Ben Bulben crest,

they found Angus Ōg standing in grief over Dearmid's body, with all his folk behind him; the tall Danann warriors holding their shields hind-side forward in token of peace. And as Grania's people drew near, Angus lifted his head and asked them what they had come for.

'The Princess Grania has sent us to fetch home the body of her lord,' said they.

But Angus said, 'Grania had him while he lived, and it is because of her he died. Now, what is left of him comes with me to Brugh-Na-Boyna, for that is his home.'

And he gave orders for Dearmid's body to be placed on a golden bier, with his javelins fixed point upward on either side. And his people rested the bier on their shoulders, and carried it slowly away towards Brugh-Na-Boyna.

For a while, Grania continued her life alone, grieving for her lost lord, and teaching her sons to hate Finn Mac Cool for their father's death. But her heart was not made for hopeless sorrow, and before three summers were past, her grief began to fade. Then Finn came to her again. At first she met him with bitter scorn, but he knew how to wait, and was so patient in his waiting, so gentle and loving-kind, that at last she began to soften towards him. And the day came when she made peace between him and her sons, and returned with him as his bride, to Almu of the White Walls.

But when he brought her in through the gate, the Fianna burst into bitter laughter. 'A bad bargain have you made, Finn Mac Cool, for Dearmid was worth a hundred of this one!'

And Fergus Finvel said, 'Better keep her tied to the roof tree, lest she run off with the next man to catch her eye, seeing there is so little faith in her!'

And though, after the first ugly greeting, the Fianna treated Grania always as befitted Finn's wife, there was coldness between them and her always, for Dearmid's sake.

Nevertheless, Finn's wife she remained, until the last day of his life.

14
The Battle of Gavra

Cormac Mac Art the High King died.

And Cairbri of the Liffey, his son, set his foot on the Crowning Stone in the midst of the High Court at Tara, and standing so, with one foot on the Stone and the other on a red bull's hide, he was crowned High King of Erin in his father's place. And Finn with the Fian chiefs and champions stood by, on one side, facing the warriors of the King's household standing on the other, and raised three great shouts of triumph and of greeting for the new High King.

But Finn's heart was heavy under his bronze breast-armour, and a shadow lay on his mind, for he knew Cairbri had always hated him and the Clan Bascna.

Now Cairbri had a daughter called Sgeimh Solais, which means Light of Beauty. And indeed she was well named, for though scarcely yet out of her child-hood, she was already the fairest thing in all Erin, more fair even than Grania had been at her age. And many great chiefs and nobles and even kings from across the seas came seeking her in marriage. And at last, after many others had failed — for this princess too was hard to please — a marriage was arranged between her and the King's son of the Decies, and a great wedding feast was made ready.

It was the custom that when any princess of the royal house of Tara went to her wedding, the High King should give the Fianna a tribute of twenty ingots of gold. And the way of it was this: that when the nine days' wedding feast was about to begin, the chiefs of the Fianna sent their youngest and most newly-joined warrior into the High King's hall to claim the tribute, and themselves waited for his return in their encampment on the broad green before the palace.

But Cairbri of the Liffey hated not only Finn and the Clan Bascna, for Dearmid's sake, but he hated the whole Fianna, for under Finn' captaincy they had grown to be a great power in the land; and Cairbri was afraid that the time might come when they would be stronger than the High King. He had long been looking for a chance to break them, and now it seemed to him that the chance was come . . .

The Fianna in their encampment waited long and long for the return of young Ferdia with the royal slaves bearing the gold. He came at last, but not out through the gates with the gold-bearers behind him. He came alone and over the ramparts, falling all arms and legs, heavy as a dead man falls. And when they ran forward and stood about him they saw the spear wound over his heart. And the voice of Cairbri's herald called down to them from the ramparts: 'Hear the words of the High King of Erin: "There have been over-many demands from the Fianna in my father's time; take now from me the answer that I make to all such, now that I, Cairbri, am the High King." '

They brought the boy's body to Finn and told him the words of Cairbri Mac Cormac.

And Finn stood up and swore a mighty and terrible oath. 'The High King's answer is received and laid to heart. I, Finn Mac Cool the Lord of the Fianna, have laid it *close* to heart. And now I swear on my father's head, that never again while I am its Captain, shall there be peace between the High King and the Fianna of Erin!'

Then the Fianna of Clan Bascna shouted their wrath and beat with their spears upon their shields. And many shouted to Finn to lead them at once in storming the Royal Hill of Tara. But Fer-tai, the Fian Chief of Tara and the Meath men, who was marriage-kin to Goll Mac Morna, rose and stood over against him with the Clan Morna at his back, and called on them to hold by the High King and not by Finn Mac Cool. So fighting broke out between Clan Bascna and Clan Morna, and the old feud that had slept so long woke and raged forth like a forest fire.

But Cairbri, seeing from the walls of Tara the fighting in the Fian camp, knew that the two clans were too nearly matched; and he had need of the Clan Morna chieftains. So he sent his swiftest messenger running to them with word to break off the fight and fall back within the walls of the Royal Hill. Then the Clan Morna chiefs under Fer-tai broke off the fight, and fell back, while the King's own household warriors manned the ramparts to cover their retreat with a hail-storm of spears.

Then, seeing that to push after them would be to run upon disaster, Finn sounded his horn to recall his own men. And that sunset, without pausing even to break the camp, Finn ordered the standard of the Fianna to be raised and they marched South to join themselves to Fercob, King of Munster, who was marriage-kin to Finn Mac Cool, even as was Cairbri, but a friend and sworn comrade beside.

They sent runners ahead to warn Fercob, and as they went, they called on the main body of the Fianna to gather to the Munster hosting-plain.

And in like manner, Cairbri sent out his runners, summoning them, and the kings of all the Provinces, to muster to him at Tara. And the Clan Morna and the kings of Ulster and Connacht and even Finn's own Leinster mustered to Tara. But Fercob of Munster gathered his spears to fight beside Finn, and the Clan Bascna were with them there.

The sound of armourers' hammers on anvils rang from shore to shore of Erin, and the *whitt-whitt-whitt* of weapons on weapon-stones in the forecourts of chief and captain; and the very ground trembled under the tramp of feet as the warriors gathered to Cairbri or to Finn.

Then the fighting began, and the ding of hammer on anvil became the clash of blade on blade where the war-bands met in small fierce weapon-flurries, trying each other's strength. Then, as streamlets flow into a stream and the streams flow at last into the Shannon or the slow strong Boyne, the small fights became greater ones, and at last the two war hosts came to face each other on the bare sunny moors of Gavra for the last battle that must settle all things between them.

On the night before the battle the watchfires of the hosts were as though the stars had fallen from the sky in two great scattered swathes of light, and between them the moor was an emptiness of dark. When the morning came, the two war hosts took up their battle array, and between them the moor stretched empty to the wind and sunlight, and murmurous with bees.

On the one side, Cairbri the High King stood

beneath his silken standard, and behind him and on either side stretched the war host of Tara, company by company under their chieftains. Fer-tai and Fir-li his son captained the Clan Morna and all of the Fianna that stood with them, and the kings of the provinces each with their warriors, and close around the High King the five sons of Urgriu of the ancient tribes of Tara, each leading one of the 'Pillars' of the High King's own household troops.

And on the other side the war host was drawing up in three parts, and in the centre the King of Munster commanded all the fighting-strength of his province, while the Fianna of Clan Bascna and such as had joined them were drawn up on the wings. Osca commanded the left wing, and the leader of the right (the post which in all battles carries the most of honour and of danger) was Finn Mac Cool himself.

The Fian Captain had put on his whole splendour of war gear; a silk shirt next his skin, and over it a battle shirt of many layers of linen waxed together, and over that his tunic of fine-meshed ringmail, and over that his gold-bordered belly-armour. Round his waist, a belt clasped with golden dragon heads; his sword hung at his side, his blue-bladed Lochlan war spear was in his hand; on his shoulder his round shield covered with green leather, its boss enriched with flowers of gold and silver and bronze. On his head, his war-cap of gilded bronze set about the brow with mountain gems that sparked back yellow-tawny light in the early rays of the sun. And around him the Clan Bascna stood close — shoulder to shoulder and shield to shield under their bright-tipped spears.

The war horns sounded, and the two war hosts

rushed upon each other. As they drew close together, the throwing-spears began to hum to and fro, and the moor of Gavra shook beneath their running feet, and from both sides the war cries and the Dord Fian rose like the surf of a mighty sea. And when they came together, the crash of their meeting rang through the Five Provinces of Erin and echoed back from the cold outer circle of the sky.

Then many a spear was broken, and many a bright blade shattered into crimsoned shards, and many a shield and war-cap hacked in two, and many a champion cut down into his own blood, and many a dead face turned towards the sky. And the young heather grew purple-red as though it were in flower a month before its time.

Osca was the spearhead of the attack that day, and wherever he turned his spear it seemed that a hundred warriors fell before him, opening a broad path for his following, into the boiling heart of the battle.

And so he came at last, with his wounds blazing red upon him, to where Cairbri fought at the head of his household warriors. Cairbri leapt to meet him, and there among all the turmoil of the battle, they fought as though they had been alone in all the sunny uplands of Gavra. Again and again they wounded each other sore, but neither felt the sting of wounds that would have slain lesser men three times over, until at last Osca got in a blow that entered Cairbri's body where the upper and lower plates of his belly armour came together, and drove out again through the small of his back. But as the High King fell, his falling twisted the spear from Osca's grasp, and from the ground he thrust up at him, so that the spear entered below his guard and pierced upward from his belly into his breast. The blood came into his mouth, and he pitched forward across the High King's body, with the pains of death already upon him.

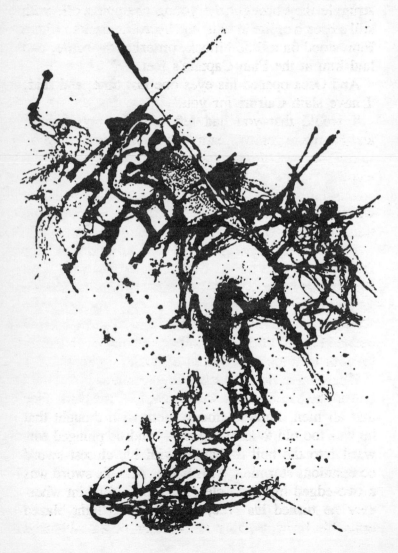

Then Cairbri's household warriors charged forward to get possession of their lord's body, and the champion's who had slain him. But those who followed Osca did the same and after sharp and bitter struggle they brought the young champion off, with still a breath of life in him, and bore him back to where Finn stood on a little hillock, ordering the battle, and laid him at the Fian Captain's feet.

And Osca opened his eyes one last time, and said, 'I have slain Cairbri for you.'

'I would that you had left him for my slaying, and for me to get my death from him, instead of you,' said Finn, and for the second time in his life, he wept.

'Do not be doing that for me,' Osca said, 'for if it were you lying there, and I standing over you, do you think it's one tear I'd be weeping for you?'

'I know well enough that you would not, for Dearmid O'Dyna stands between us even now,' said Finn. 'But as for me, I will weep for whom I choose to weep for!'

And with the thing part in jest and part in sorrow between them, Osca died. And there was not a palm's breadth of his body without a wound on it.

'That was a hero's death,' said Finn.

And the battle frenzy woke in him — the battle fury that all men, himself among them, had thought that he was too old to know again — and he plunged forward into the boil of battle, with his closest sword companions storming at his heels. And his sword was a two-edged lightning clearing a path for him wherever he turned his face, and the hero light blazed upon his brow, so that no warrior could withstand him, and the dead fell in tangled heaps about him; and he thrust over them and through them like a young bull through standing barley. But as he went, one after another of the men behind him fell, Dering and Keelta and Coil Croda and Fincel and Ligan Lummina until he was raging alone through the enemy war host. And Fer-li the son of Fer-tai, saw him with no friend to guard his back, and made at him with drawn sword, for both their spears were gone long since; and so they fought until both were sore wounded. But at the last Finn swung up his sword for a mighty blow, and struck Fer-li's head from his shoulders so that it went rolling and bouncing away under the feet of the battle, and Finn Mac Cool had the victory in *that* fight.

But after, Fer-tai came hurling himself upon him to avenge his son.

'Great deeds, Finn!' he shouted. 'Great deeds to be slaying a boy!'

'Not so much a boy. And if you felt him so young and helpless, why did you not come before?' Finn mocked him.

'I had hoped that he would finish the slaying. I had rather that he had the pride and the honour of it!'

So they fought across Fer-li's headless body, knee to knee and shield to shield, and over their shield and under their armour, the blood ran down. And at last Finn slew the father as he had slain the son.

And as he stood over the bodies, panting and far spent, and half blind with blood, the five sons of Urgriu came upon him in a circle, and Finn turned about and saw them all round him, closing in with spears raised to strike; and he knew that the end was come. He let his shield that could not face five ways at once drop to his feet, and stood straight and unmoving as a pillar-stone.

And the five spears came at him, making five great wounds that put out the light of the sun . . .

15
The Return of Oisīn

In the Valley of the Thrushes, not far from where Dublin stands today, a crowd of men were trying to shift a great boulder from their tilled land, the village headman directing their efforts. The stone had been there as long as any of them could remember, or their grandfathers before them, and always they had grumbled at it because it got in the way of the ploughing. But though one or two half-hearted attempts had been made to shift it, it still lay half embedded in the hill side, where it always had lain.

Now at last, they were really set upon getting rid of the thing, and every man in the village had gathered to lend his strength to the task.

But it seemed that their strength was all too little, for there they were heaving and straining and grunting and hauling, their faces crimson and the sweat running off them, and the great boulder not moving so much as a finger's breadth out of its bed.

And as they strained and struggled — and they getting nearer each moment to giving up — they saw riding towards them a horseman such as none of them had ever set eyes on before, save maybe in some glorious dream. Taller and mightier than any man of this world he was, and riding a foam-white stallion as far beyond mortal horses as he was beyond mortal men. His eyes were strangely dark, his fair hair like a sunburst about his head. A mantle of saffron silk flowed back from brooches of yellow gold that clasped it at his shoulders, and at his side hung a great golden-hilted sword.

'It is one of the Fairy Kind!' said an aged villager, making the sign of the horns with the first two fingers of his left hand.

'It is an archangel out of heaven!' said a young one, and made the sign of the Cross.

The splendid being, man or fairy or angel, reined in his horse, and sat looking down at them with a puzzled pity on his face. 'You wanted this shifting?' he said.

The headman drew nearer, greatly daring. 'We did so, but it seems 'tis beyond our strength. Would you be lending us the power of your arm, now?'

'Surely,' said the rider, and stooping from the saddle, set his hand under the boulder and gave a mighty heave. The boulder came out of the ground and went rolling over and over down the hillside like a shinty ball, and the watching villagers gave a great shout of wonder and admiration. But next moment their shouts turned to fearful and wondering dismay.

For as he heaved at the boulder the rider's saddle girth had burst, so that he fell headlong to the ground. The moment the white stallion felt himself free, he neighed three times and set off at a tearing gallop towards the coast, and as he went, he seemed not merely to grow small with distance, but to lose shape and substance and fade into the summer air like a wisp of wood-smoke.

And there on the ground, where the splendid stranger had fallen, lay an old, old man, huge still, but with thin white beard and milky half-blind eyes, his silken mantle a patched and tattered cloak of coarsest homespun, his golden-hilted sword a rough ash stick such as a blind old beggar might use to support him and feel his way about the world. He half raised himself and peered about, then with a wild despairing cry, stretched all his length again burying his head in his arms.

In a little, seeing that nothing terrible seemed to have happened to any of themselves, some of the bolder of the villagers came closer and lifted him up and asked him who he was.

'I am Oisīn the son of Finn Mac Cool,' said the old man.

Then the villagers looked at each other, and the headman said, 'If you mean who I think you mean, then you're as crazy as we must have been just now to be taking you for whatever it was we took you for.'

'It was the sun in our eyes,' said another man.

And they asked the old man a second time who he was.

'Why do you ask again, when I have already told you? I am Oisīn the son of Finn Mac Cool, Captain of the Fianna of Erin.'

'It is the sun on that bald head of yours,' said the headman, kindly enough. 'Finn Mac Cool and his heroes we have heard of, yes, but they have been dead these three hundred years.'

Then the old man was silent a long while, his face bowed into his hands. At last he said, 'How did they die?'

'At the Battle of Gavra, not so far from here at all. There is a green mound up there beside the battle-ground. I was hearing once it was the grave of one of them, called Osca. A great battle it was, and they do say that there were none but boys and old men left in Erin when the fighting was done.'

'But Oisīn did not die then,' another put in. 'No man knows the death of Oisīn, but the harpers still sing the songs he made.'

'But now Priest Patrick has come into Erin, and told us of the one true God, and Christ His Son, and the old days are done with, and we listen to them only as men listen to old tales that are half forgotten.'

The old man seemed half-dazed, like one that has taken a blow between the eyes. Only he cried out once, harshly and near to choking, 'Strong and without mercy is your new God! And He has much to answer for if He has slain the memory of Finn and Osca!'

Then the people were angry and cried 'Sacrilege!' and some of them picked up the small surface stones of the field to throw at the old man. But the headman bade them let him be until Priest Patrick had seen him and told them what they should do.

So they took him to the old fortress of Drum Derg, where Patrick had at that time made his living place.

And Patrick listened to their account of how he had come to them, and how, with the sun in their eyes they had mistaken him for a young man and asked his aid in moving the great stone from their tilled land, and of what had happened after.

And Patrick was kind to the huge half-blind old beggar, and gave him a place for sleeping and a place for sitting by the fire, among his own Christian brotherhood.

And often the priest of the new God, and the old man who had been Oisīn would talk together. And Oisīn told wonderful stories — almost all the stories that are in this book and many more beside — of Finn and the Fianna and the High and Far-off Days, which Patrick bade one of his scribes to write down on pages of fair white sheepskin, lest they should be forgotten.

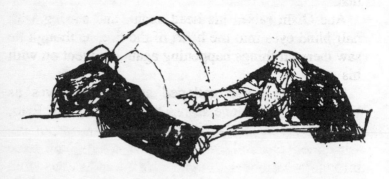

As time went by, Patrick came to believe that the old man was indeed Oisīn the son of Finn Mac Cool, and one day he said to him, 'It is upward of three hundred years since Finn and Osca and the flower of the Fianna died at Gavra. Tell me then, how is it that you have lived so long beyond your day and the days of your companions?'

So Oisīn told him this last story: the story of how he had ridden hunting with the Fianna one summer morning among the lakes of Killarney, and how the Princess Niamh of the Golden Hair had come out of the West, and asked him to return to Tyr-na-nOg with her. And how he had taken leave of Finn and Osca and the rest, and mounted behind her on her white horse, and how they had headed westward again until they came to the sea, and headed westward still, leaving the companions of the Fianna behind them on the shore.

And when he reached that point in his story, Oisīn buried his face in his hands and seemed to forget.

Then, to rouse him, and because he was a man of curiosity and interest in all things, Patrick said, 'Success and benediction! Tell me what happened after that.'

And Oisīn raised his head again, and staring with half-blind eyes into the heart of the fire, as though he saw there all things happening again, he went on with his story.

'The white horse galloped across the waves as lightly as he had done across the green hills of Erin, and the wind overtook the waves, and we overtook the wind, and presently we passed into a golden haze through which there loomed half-seen islands with cities on their heights and palaces among leafy gardens. Once a fallow doe fled past us, chased by a milk-white hound with one blood-red ear; and once a maiden fled by on a bay horse, and she carrying a golden apple in her hand, and close behind her in hot pursuit, a young man on a white steed, a purple and crimson cloak flying from his shoulders, and a great sword naked in his hand.

'But the sky began to darken overhead, and the wind rose and began to blow in great gusts that roused the waves to fury and sent the spindrift flying like white birds over our heads, and the lightning leapt between the dark sky and darker sea, while the thunder boomed and crashed all about us. Yet still the white horse sped on, unafraid, as lightly and sweetly as over the summer seas that we had traversed before. And presently the wind died and the darkness rolled away and sunshine touched the racing seas with gold. And ahead of us, under the spreading lake of blue sky, lay the fairest land that ever I had seen. Green plains and distant hills were all bathed in a honey-wash of sunlight that .flashed and sparkled from the lakes and streams that met every turn of the eye, and changed to gold the white walls of the beautiful palace which stood close beside the shore. Flowers were everywhere, and butterflies like dancing flames upon the air, and as soon as I saw it, I knew that this could be no place but Tyr-na-nOg, the Land of Youth.

'The white horse skimmed the waves towards the shore, and on the white sand we dismounted, and Niamh turned to me, most sweetly holding out her hands, and said, "This is my own land. Everything I promised, you shall find here, and above all and before all, the love of Niamh of the Golden Hair."

'Then there came towards us from the palace a troop of warriors, heroes and champions all, holding their shields reversed in token to me that they came in peace. And after them a gay and beautiful company led by the King of the land himself, in a robe of yellow silk, a golden crown blazing like the midsummer sun upon his head. And behind him came the Queen, most fair to see, and with a hundred maidens clustered all about her.

'They kissed their daughter joyfully and tenderly, and the King took my hand in his saying, "A hundred thousand welcomes, brave Oisín." Then turning with me to face all the host, he said, "This is Oisín, from the far-off land of Erin, he who is to be husband of Niamh of the Golden Hair. Bid him welcome, as I do."

'Then all the hosts, nobles and warriors and maidens alike bade me welcome. And all together, Niamh and myself walking hand in hand in their midst, we went up to the palace, where a great feast was prepared.

'For ten days and nights we feasted, while the harpers made music sweeter than any heard in the world of men. I, Oisín, say that, I who was a harper among harpers of the world of men, in my time — and little birds as brightly coloured as flowers flew and fluttered about the banquet-house. And on the tenth day, Niamh and I were wed.

'I lived in the Land of Youth three years — I thought it was three years — and I was happy as never man was happy before. But as the third year drew to a close, I began to think more and more of my father and my son, and of all the companions of my youth. Sometimes as we rode hunting, I would fancy that I heard the Fian hunting horn echoing through the woods, and think I recognized the deep baying of Bran and Skolawn among the belling of the milk-white Danann hounds. I began to fall into waking dreams, thinking how they would be hunting the woods of Slieve Bloom, of how the heroes would be telling old stories about the fire, in Almu of the White Walls, until it came to this — that Niamh asked me if I no longer loved her. I told her that she was the very life of my heart, and that I was happy as ever I had been in the Land of Youth, but the restlessness was on me, and I longed to see my father and my friends once more.

'Then Niamh kissed me and clung to me, and tried to turn my thoughts elsewhere. But still I half-heard the Fian hunting horn echoing through my dreams at night, and at last I begged leave of her and of the King her father, to visit my own land once more.

'The King gave me leave, though unwillingly, and Niamh said, "It's not that I can be holding you while your heart draws you back to Erin, so I give you my leave also, though there's a shadow on my mind, and I fear that I shall never see you again."

'I said, "That is a foolish fear, for there's nothing that could keep me long from you. Only give me the white steed, for he knows the way and will bring me back safely to your side."

'Then she said, "I will give you the white steed, for indeed he knows the way. But listen now, and keep my words in your mind. Never once dismount from his back all the while you are in the world of men, for if you do, you can never come back to me. If once your feet touch the green grass of Erin, the way back to Tyr-na-nOg will be closed to you for ever."

'I promised that I would never dismount from the white steed, but remember always her words. And seeing her grief, which even my most faithful promise seemed not to touch, I was within a feather-weight of yielding to her and remaining always in Tyr-na-nOg; but the white horse stood ready, and the hunger was still on me, to see my father and my own land.

'So I mounted, and the horse set off at a gallop towards the shore. So again we sped across the sea, and the wind overtook the waves and we overtook the wind, and the shores of the Land of Youth sank into the golden mist behind us.

'Again it drifted all about us, that golden mist, and in the mist the towers and cities of the sea arose once more. And again the maiden with the golden apple in her hand fled past us on her bay horse, and the young horseman riding hard behind, his purple cloak streaming from his shoulders and his sword naked in his hand. And again the fallow doe fled by, hunted by the milk-white hound with one ear red as blood.

'So we came at last to the green shores of Erin.

'Gladly, once we were on land, I turned the horse's head towards Almu of the White Walls and rode on. And as I rode, I looked about me, seeking for familiar scenes and faces, and listening always for the sound of the Fian hunting horn. But all things seemed strangely altered, and nowhere did I hear or see any sign of my companions, and the folk who were tilling the ground were small and puny, so that they did not seem any more like countrymen of mine.

'I came at last through the woods to the open country around the Hill of Almu, and the hill was still there but overgrown with bushes and brambles, and on its broad flat crest, where the white walls of my father's dun had used to rise with its byres and barns and armourers' shops, the women's court and the guest quarters, and Finn's mighty mead-hall rising in the midst of all, were nothing but grassy hummocks grown over with elder and blackthorn and the arched sprays of the brambles, and the heather washing over all.

'Then horror fell upon me — though indeed I believed then that the dun was still there, but hidden from me by some enchantment of the Danann folk. And I flung wide my arms and shouted the names of Finn my father and Osca, and after them, the names of all the old brotherhood, Keelta, and Conan and Dering and the rest. Even Dearmid's name I shouted in that dreadful time. But no one answered, nothing moved save a thrush fluttering among the elder bushes. Then I thought that perhaps the hounds might hear me when men could not, and I shouted to Bran and Skolawn and strained my ears for an answering bark. But no sound came, save the hushing of a little wind through the hilltop grasses.

'So with the horror thick upon me, I wheeled the white horse and rode away from Almu, to search all Erin until I found my friends again, or some way out of the enchantment that held me captive. But everywhere I rode, I met only little puny people who gazed at me in wonder out of the faces of strangers, and in every household of the Fianna the brambles grew and the birds were at their nesting. So at last I came to the Glen of the Thrushes, where often I had hunted with Finn, and saw before me tilled land where I remembered only forest.

'And at the head of the tilled land a knot of these small and puny strangers were striving to shift a great stone that was in the way of ploughing. I rode close, and they asked me for my help. And that was an easy thing to give, so I stooped in the saddle and set my hand under the stone and sent it rolling down the hillside. But with the strain of the heave my saddle girth broke, and I was flung to the ground, and my feet were on the green grass of Erin.

'Priest Patrick, the rest of my story they have told you!'

THE WOLVES OF WILLOUGHBY CHASE

JOAN AIKEN

She woke suddenly to find that the train had stopped with a jerk.
'Oh! What is it? Where are we?' she exclaimed before she could stop herself.
'No need to alarm yourself, miss,' said her companion. 'Wolves on the line,
most likely – they often have trouble of that kind hereabouts.'
'Wolves!' Sylvia stared at him in terror.

After braving a treacherous journey through snow-covered wastes populated by packs of wild and hungry wolves, Sylvia joins her cousin Bonnie in the warmth and safety of Willoughby Chase. But with Bonnie's parents overseas and the evil Miss Slighcarp left in charge, the cousins soon find their human predators even harder to escape.

'Joan Aiken is such a spellbinder that it all rings true...'
THE STANDARD

ISBN 0099411865 £4.99

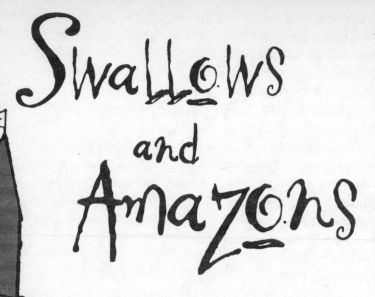

Swallows
and
Amazons

Arthur Ransome

Titty drew a long breath that nearly choked her.
'It is...' she said.
The flag blowing in the wind at the masthead of the little boat was
black and on it in white were a skull and two crossed bones.
The four on the island stared at each other.

To John, Susan, Titty and Roger, being allowed to use the boat *Swallow* to go camping on the island is adventure enough. But they soon find themselves under attack from the fierce Amazon Pirates, Nancy and Peggy. And so begins a summer of battles, alliances, exploration and discovery.

By the winning author of the first Carnegie medal.

ISBN 0099503913   £4.99